The Mysterious Marksman

The Mysterious Marksman
Seno Gumira Ajidarma
First published in Indonesian under the title *Penembak Misterius*
by PT. Pustaka Utama Grafiti, Jakarta, 1993
First edition © 2019 The Lontar Foundation
Copyright for English-language translations © 2019 Joan Suyenaga
Copyright to the original Indonesian texts held by the author
Copyright to this edition © 2019 The Lontar Foundation
All rights reserved including the rights of reproduction
in whole or in part in any form.

No part of this publication may be reproduced
or transmitted in any form or by any means
without permission in writing from
The Lontar Foundation
Jl. Danau Laut Tawar No. 53
Jakarta 10210 Indonesia
www.lontar.org

Publication of this title was made possible by the generous assistance of Toeti Heraty.

Template design by DesignLab; layout and cover by Cyprianus Jaya Napiun
Cover illustration: *Terdampar di Kebun Sang Mata-Mata*
(Abandoned in a Forest of Spies) by I Made Arya Palguna
Image courtesy of the Oei Hong Djien Museum of Contemporary Art.
The tatoo reproduced on page 17, 19, 20, 21, were designed by
the tatoo artist, Samsul "Tato Malioboro"

ISBN 978-602-6978-83-7

MODERN LIBRARY OF INDONESIA

SENO GUMIRA AJIDARMA

The Mysterious Marksman

short stories

translated by
Joan Suyenaga

Jakarta, Indonesia

bang!

tattooed corpse
dumped in the river

splash!

Indonesian haiku – 1983

Contents

The Mysterious Marksman Trilogy:
The Obsession with Tattooed Corpses

I.
The Mysterious Marksman

II.
Stories For Alina

III.
Whose Baby is Crying in the Bushes?

The Mysterious Marksman Trilogy:
THE OBSESSION WITH TATTOOED CORPSES

Seno Gumira Ajidarma

My friends,

You have asked about "obsession and process" in regards to how I write my short stories. This question resembles, but is not identical to, the task I was given one year ago: to explain the creative process behind the birth of four of my short stories that were selected for the anthology of stories that appeared in the daily national newspaper, *Kompas*, in 1992, *Pelajaran Mengarang* [*Writing Lessons*].[1] The difference between these two questions is that the former task was more specific; it applied to only those four stories. This task is perhaps more general, seeking a kind of overall formula—that is, in fact, impossible. Why?

First, to concoct a justifiable formula one would have to analyze *all* of my short stories. Second, a formula about "obsession and the writing process" of all of those stories is impossible because each short story has its own process, each one is unique. What's more, the creative process is actually mysterious—the cause and

---

[1] *About Four Short Stories*, paper discussed in the program, Garden Seminar, at IKIP Muhammadiyah Jakarta, in Kebun Raya Bogor, November 28, 1993. Reprinted in *Basis*, July 1994.

the result are saturated with the X factor: it cannot be rationalized. In the series of books, *Proses Kreatif Mengapa dan Bagaimana Saya Mengarang* [The Creative Process: Why and How I Write],[2] we find a wide variety of accounts of writers' creative processes.

So, what will we talk about today? Perhaps I will address the key word, obsession. Do I have an obsession? Actually, every short story, or every piece of work, is born of an obsession: something that persistently occupies the mind. However, to be more specific today, I will speak about obsession in regards to three of my stories: *The Keroncong Killing, The Sound of Rain on the Roof,* and *Grrrh!* These three short stories were published in an anthology, *The Mysterious Marksman*, and were combined under one sub-heading, *The Mysterious Marksman: a Trilogy.*[3] This indicates that indeed there was a red thread in the birth of these three stories—there was an "obsession". And so, we have a topic for discussion.

My friends,

In 1983, the newspapers were filled with stories about the findings of tattooed corpses in public areas. These corpses were sprawled everywhere—some with their hands tied together, some without; all of them with bullet wounds. And these corpses were instantly identified: they were the *gali* (short for *gang anak liar,* wild boys gang)— individuals that the civilized world labelled as "criminals". Reports in the mass media were limited to the appearances of these corpses. Or their names. Or the way the corpses were found. Or—and these were the most intriguing—

---

[2] Pamusuk Eneste edited a series of three books with this title. The first two books in the series were published by Gramedia; I have forgotten about the third book. (**Note:** book #3 was published by KPG, published in 1986 and 2009; book #4 was published by KPG, 2009. The series of four books were published together by KPG in 2009.)

[3] Seno Gumira Ajidarma, *Penembak Misterius* [*The Mysterious Marksman*], (Jakarta: Pustaka Utama Grafiti, 1993), pp. 3-36.

sometimes there were eyewitness accounts: corpses thrown out in the middle of the day in the middle of a busy crowd, a market for instance, from a jeep that quickly disappeared. These corpses were referred to as the victims of *Petrus*—an abbreviation of *Penembak Misterius [Mysterious Marksman]*.

This phenomenon was controversial. On the one hand, those who had felt threatened by these criminals, the *gali*, seemed to be relieved. The *gali* at that time had become a kind of mafia who were fearfully obeyed. They operated in their own territories where no one dared to oppose them, while money for "security guarantees" flowed into their pockets. Lower and middle-class merchants were clearly happy that the *gali* were being slaughtered. The populace had long suffered at the hands of these violent criminals: grandmothers slashed, wives raped in front of their husbands, rampant thefts along with torture. Suddenly, it was "safe" to walk outside of the house at night. At least for a while.

In his autobiography, President Soeharto referred to this situation and expressed his concern. He felt that the solution to this problem required *shock therapy*.[4] This statement could be interpreted as a justification for these mysterious shootings. In other words, it would appear that the Mysterious Marksman was a state agent. However, this extra-judicial eradication of criminals was not an official state act.

In fact, this sentiment led to strong reactions. These killings were seen as violations of the law. Legal experts argued that the death sentence could be enforced only after the *gali* had been tried and sentenced in a court of law. Other critics declared that the killings were not effective because as long as poverty existed, there would always be people who resorted to committing crimes.

---

[4] G. Dwipayana and Ramadhan KH, *Soeharto, Pikiran, Ucapan, dan Tindakan Saya [Soeharto: My Thoughts, Words and Actions]*, (Jakarta: PT Citra Lamtoro Gung Persada, 1989), pp. 389-391.

I remember most clearly when Arief Budiman wrote an article in *Kompas* about a robbery committed during the flag-raising ceremony on Bhayangkara Day, a day to commemmorate the police force. I forget where the event occurred, perhaps Bandung, but I distinctly remember the conclusion: "Fear has its limits". Indeed, this robbery occurred in the midst of the commotion of the mysterious shootings. This is one critical perspective: the mysterious killings did not provide an exit route.

My friends,

For me, this entire situation meant only one thing: drama. The corpses were scattered in all directions—even though I never saw one myself—and the gossip was incessant and overflowing because the news was so limited. There were many versions, many histories, many "short stories", beginning with stories about captures to disturbing stories about killings of people who had already relented their crimes. When the alleged coup of September 30, 1965, and the subsequent killings happened, I was too young to think critically. So, for me, the eradication of these criminals between 1983-1985 was my first "big event". Besides that, I had my own ideas about these *gali*.

I had known the word *gali*—I don't know why they were called that—since I was young in Yogyakarta. As a "normal" youth, I spent my days and nights on the streets. In my youthful eyes, through which everything appeared bright and shiny, these *gali* looked like heroes, like reckless champions. They displayed attributes that boasted of their prowess: wellbuilt bodies, dark glasses, felt hats, boots, and the respect of everyone around them. Actually, to this day, I have never seen these *gali* in action, in a physical brawl. But, my scanty impression, influenced by the stories of their "big names" and of course, my imagination—idealization, to be exact—made these *gali* into champions in my eyes; champions who we could call upon for help at any moment.

So, when the execution of these *gali* happened several years later I was deeply affected. My image of these *gali* had become a part of my life history. When they were exterminated like cockroaches, it seemed as if a part of me had been wiped away. This, by itself, influenced the mechanism of my writing. Every day, I wondered: what else can be written, what else can be written …

My friends,

The short story, "The Keroncong Killing", perhaps seems distant from the factual events of the mysterious killings. The story is about a Mysterious Marksman that was hired to assassinate someone at a party. His target is a member of the opposition. In the end, the Mysterious Marksman seems to aim for the person who ordered the assassination.

This short story was written as a first person narrative in an attempt to understand the psychology of the Mysterious Marksman. Another part of me undertook a critical attitude and rejected the order to kill. To remind readers of the realities of the Mysterious Marksman, I added this dialog:

> "*I don't want to shoot innocent people.*"
> "*That's none of your business. Last year you shot thousands of innocent people.*"[5]

This short story was first published on February 3, 1985. "Last year" could mean either 1984 or 1983, because the gossip that I heard was that the mysterious killings continued with the number of victims reaching the thousands. By "innocent", of course, I mean "untried".

---

[5] Ajidarma, *op. cit.*, p. xx.

When this story was first going to be published in the newspaper, *Kompas*, the editors requested that the word "batik" be dropped from the description of the clothes that the assassin's target was wearing. They claimed that by eliminating the word "batik", "this event could happen anywhere, not just in Indonesia". Thus, in the short story, all references to "batik" were dropped, except for one instance. However, when the story was published in an anthology, I reinstated the word "batik". This event shows that I missed my target, but I hit something else. To be frank, this short story is more of an exercise in building tension in the reader.

The second story, "The Sound of Rain on the Roof", is clearly closer to the topic. It tells of a woman named Sawitri, who is waiting for her boyfriend, who is a *gali*. She is terrified as she waits because every time the rain subsides, a tattooed body is always thrown out at the entrance to the alley. Whenever the rain subsides, Sawitri always opens the window and peers to her right to see if, who knows—and please let it not be—her boyfriend who is thrown out in front of the alley. That is why she is always afraid to hear the rain on the roof tiles.

> *At first, the bodies were thrown out on to the streets at any time. Morning, noon, evening, night. Bodies strewn in the corners of the market, floating in the rivers, buried in the gutters, or splayed out on the highways. Every day, the newspapers would print photos of tattooed corpses with gun wounds in the neck, forehead, heart, or between the eyes. Occasionally, a tattooed body would be thrown onto the main street in the middle of the day from a car that quickly vanished. The bodies that fell into the middle of a crowd caused a big commotion.*[6]

---

[6] *Ibid.*, p. xx.

Aren't these sentences a repetition of what I described above? This short story was finished on July 15, 1985, when the newspapers had stopped publishing stories about the tattooed corpses. Clearly, this is a picture that was seared in my brain—an obsession: something I thought about constantly, until it found its way into a short story.

In this story, I retain one perspective. Concretely, Sawitri's perspective remains at her window. Abstractly, Sawitri can only speculate what has happened to her boyfriend. Imaginatively, both of these perspectives are mine. The repetition of Sawitri opening her window every time the rain subsides and peering to her right to look for the tattooed corpse perhaps reflects that obsession. I can envision all of this in my mind.

This obsession became more real when, in December 1986, I finished the story, "Grrrh!" This unremitting obsession allowed me to master aspects of the phenomenon so that I could write about it in the absurd: what if the tattooed corpses rose from their graves and took their revenge? To have these living corpses succeed in causing mayhem, even though they could be exterminated by missiles, shows my sympathies with them because of the injustice, to be exact, that they had been executed without being tried in court for their crimes.

Of course, I showed that I was referring to the mysterious killings in Indonesian history.

> *"Don't you remember? Along with Ngadul, six thousand third-class criminals were secretly wiped out! Do you remember, sir?"*
>
> *"Yes, yes! Why?"*
>
> *"Most of the corpses were buried at the Big Hole, Commander, sir."*
>
> *"I know. So what?"*
>
> *"There's a report—many of them had retired*

from crime, sir! Many of those who were mysteriously butchered down had already reformed, sir! And no prayers were recited for them. At that time no one dared! They were afraid of being butchered too, sir, because at that time just anyone could be killed mysteriously, sir!"

Grrh! The zombie leapt from the window. Detective Sarman scaled the courtyard walls.

"So, what is your conclusion, Officer Sarman?"

"The slaughter was a big mistake, sir! Our generation is suffering the consequences! Those people weren't willing to die, sir! They're taking their revenge!"

"What do we have to do?"

"Pray for them, sir! We have to hold a mass prayer, sir! We have only one hundred missiles! That's not enough to destroy them! Pray for them, sir, so their souls will rest in peace!"[7]

When *Kompas* published this story, the editors asked me to eliminate the sentence, "The slaughter was a big mistake, sir!" I agreed. However, when the story was published in an anthology, I returned the sentence into the original text.

I wrote this story with a sense of humor and comedy, even though the images were horrifying. I borrowed the idea of a mass prayer from one of jokes Gus Dur [Abdurrahman Wahid] told at Taman Ismail Marzuki when he was the Director of the Jakarta Arts Council.

My friends,

I think that I have talked too much, especially about my own short stories. Again, I'd like to say that although the story behind the birth of a short story may be fascinating, it is the story

---

[7] *Ibid.*, pp. xx .

itself that speaks. Perhaps the notes about "obsession and process behind the writing of short stories" is appropriate only as a free-standing article, as something to be read leisurely, and does not have to be directly related with—and does not contribute anything to—the story itself.

However, upon reflection, I will note that: imagination is not capable of detaching facts from truth; it may become fiction, but it is still truth. Hopefully.

---

* "*The Mysterious Marksman* Trilogy: The Obsession with Tattooed Corpses", was read during a discussion on "Obsession and Process" at IKIP (Institut Keguruan dan Ilmu Pendidikan/Institute for Teacher Training and Pedagogy) Muhammadiyah Jakarta on December 29, 1994. It was first published in the IKIP Padang campus newspaper, *Ganto*, No. 39/V/February 1995.

I.
The Mysterious Marksman

The Keroncong Killing

it's almost night in Yogya
when my train arrives

The *keroncong* song made me sleepy, even though I had to kill someone that night. Older people like keroncong songs; the songs bear fond memories of their past.

People were scattered around down by the swimming pool; it didn't look like many of them were really listening to the music. They were talking amongst themselves. Noise and laughter burst out occasionally from every cluster.

Not everyone there was old; there were several young women. At least they were the ones who attracted my attention. I could watch them one by one through my rifle's telescope, as if I was right there amongst them. It was a lively party. They were serving roasted goat. Mmmm...

The crosshairs of my telescope continued to roam through the crowd. Once it paused on someone's forehead and moved along with him. If I pulled my trigger finger just then, he'd collapse. He would crumple slowly like a fallen tree or he would startle and disturb the laughing crowd, causing the glasses on the waiters' trays to spill. Of course, it would be even more interesting if the body fell into the pool with a splash, spraying the guests and turning the pool water red with blood. The women would scream: "Aaaarrgh!"

But I hadn't located the person I was supposed to kill. Indeed, it wasn't time yet. He would be arriving shortly. And, actually, I didn't have to go to much trouble to find him, because the person at the other end of my earphone would point him out.

"Are you ready?" I could hear the voice in the earphone. It was a sweet voice.

"I've been ready for a while. Where is he?"

"Patience. In a while."

I surveyed the crowd with my telescope from the seventh floor balcony of the hotel. The sea breeze tasted salty on my lips. Casually, while waiting for my target, I searched for the person talking to me. I watched the faces in the telescope. The women in elegant evening gowns. There were some with open backs. Gorgeous. Surely, the woman with the refined voice that was giving me instructions was beautiful. I wouldn't have suspected that a woman would be involved in an assassination like this.

"Who is my target?" I asked last week when she ordered the hit. Over the telephone, I could only imagine her face.

"You don't need to know. It's part of our contract."

This kind of contract is common. I'm paid just to shoot. The identity of my target is none of my business.

"There's one thing you can know."

"What?"

"That man's a traitor."

"A traitor?"

"A traitor of his country and nation."

So my target was a traitor of his country and nation. Would I be a hero if I shot him? I moved my rifle again. From my end of the telescope, I studied the people who were arriving. Something didn't feel right whenever I looked into the faces of the people down there.

In fact, their faces were faces of good people, but I don't know what it was that didn't feel right there. Was it that many of them were wearing official uniforms, which I despised? Or was it just my own feelings? I swore I would be really happy if my victim this time was someone loathsome. A traitor to one's country and nation was truly despicable.

I circulated my rifle through the crowd again. I was savoring this act of spying on unsuspecting people.

a pair of eyes
from behind the window

The keroncong song wasn't over yet. It seemed really long. Just like the people down there, I didn't really need to listen to it. Keroncong music now is like a museum artifact; the musicians aren't clever enough to adapt it to the changing times. Where was that woman with the velvet voice?

Everywhere people were chewing food, sipping drinks, smiling, and laughing. There were women standing stiffly next to their husbands who were busy talking while waving their hands in all directions. Men whose faces revealed they had souls of civil servants, hiding themselves in politeness but gorging themselves with food. The security officers carrying walkie-talkies were dressed in civilian clothes and paced the grounds. Apparently there were important people in attendance at this poolside, roast-goat, beach hotel party.

The night was clear and the sky was full of stars. In fact, it was a full moon. I put my rifle down because I was tired. I went into the room and got peanuts from the table. I turned the television on, but quickly turned it off again. The television programs are always terrible. The hotel room felt very quiet. I wanted to shoot my target quickly, then go home and drink a glass of beer.

"Hey, are you still there?" All of a sudden, I heard the voice again.

"Yeah, why?"

"Don't mess around! I know you're not in place!"

I quickly returned to the terrace.

"What's up? Has he arrived?"

"He's wearing a red batik shirt. It happens to be the only red shirt here, so it should be easy for you."

I looked down. There were clusters of tiny creatures. Of course, from the seventh floor, it wasn't very clear where the red batik shirt was. I lifted my rifle again. I moved into a comfortable position. While munching on the peanuts I peered through the telescope again. The crosshairs circulated again from face to face. They were still laughing and smiling. I smiled too. In a little while your faces will show unbridled fear. I can shoot all of you from here for my own satisfaction. But I won't do it. I only work on contract.

"Where is he?" I asked through the mike hanging under my chin.

"He's at the south corner of the pool, near the green umbrella."

I moved my rifle to the right. I passed by the oily faces, the smooth faces and the shiny ones. I was forced to pass by the beautiful women. And, ah, there he was. The man wearing the red batik shirt.

His face was handsome and authoritative. He was middle-aged, but didn't appear old. His hair was combed neatly to the back. He didn't laugh or smile much. People crowded around him respectfully. There were some who were playing up to him. The crosshairs of my telescope stopped exactly in the spot between his two eyes.

"Should I do it now?"

"Not yet; wait for the command!"

I watched the face. Did he have any premonitions? From this end of the telescope, at a distance, faces reflect their own characters that are different from the ones we sense when we're directly in front of the person. He didn't talk much, but it seemed that he had to answer many questions, and it appeared that he answered them very carefully. His face reflected a politeness that did not arouse any resentfulness. What would happen if I shot him? I remembered Ninoy's death in the Philippines.

But I don't know anything about politics. So, while watching the face that would soon have a hole in it, I thought about something else. Maybe he has a wife, or he has children. Or even, I thought, he could have grandchildren. They would cry upon hearing about his death, and the crying would increase when they learned about the way he died. Let it be. Wasn't he a traitor of country and nation? He deserved his sentence.

Rather stiff, I waited for the order to shoot. This was the trouble with working on contract. You couldn't do it on your own. I was paid to direct the crosshairs of my rifle's telescope to the most fatal spot, then to pull the trigger. I always told myself that I didn't kill people; I only aimed and pulled the trigger.

I looked at the face again. It felt so close, even the pores were clearly visible. It was as if I were watching the shadows of fate. In actuality, who was ending this person's life—me or You? That person had no idea that the angel of death was stroking his neck.

"How about it? Now?"

"I said to wait for the order!"

Damn that woman! How dare she yell at a paid assassin. As if acting on its own, my arm suddenly started to move the rifle. With its sixth sense, it searched through the crowd. Beautiful faces passed through my telescope. I had to bait her by talking.

"Wait for what other order?"

"You don't need to know. Just wait!"

"That's not in the contract.

"It is! Don't go off-track!"

a silk scarf
a souvenir for you

Damn! That keroncong song again, ringing in my ear. She must be near the orchestra. I searched the area around the orchestra. My telescope almost paused on the voluptuous breasts of the keroncong singer. There were several groups of people. I heard the clink of glass and dishes. Maybe she was behind the orchestra near the buffet table. There were several women and security personnel in civilian clothes. Which one? I studied them one by one. Several of them were just employees of the catering outfit. There was one woman that looked like the boss. Perhaps it was the other one. Her hair was straight and black with bangs covering her forehead. She was staring, glaring, in the direction of the red batik shirt!

"Shoot him now!" she said slowly into my headphone. I saw through my telescope that it was indeed she who spoke. It looked like it was really her. She was listening through her earphones and talking to me through a microphone hidden in her pendent. The beautiful pendent decorating her flat chest.

"What?" I asked again because I wanted to be sure it was her.

"Shoot now!"

This was how all assassinations went. A chain without a beginning or an end. This woman was surely just one link in the chain. I moved my rifle back to the target. The middle-aged man was patiently listening to someone's story. The speaker appeared agitated, but the listener seemed to restrain himself so that he too wouldn't get carried away. He nodded while looking around as if worried that someone was listening.

I was ready to shoot. One pull of my finger would end this man's life. The crosshairs of the telescope moved slightly to the side so that the bullet hole in his head would not make such a symmetrical split. My bullet would hit his left eye. And I watched his eyes closely. Oh, God. Was he really a traitor?

"You aren't mistaken? Is he really a traitor?"

"Don't ask. Shoot now!"

I looked at his eyes again. What kind of traitor?

"What kind of traitor? Why hasn't he been tried?"

"Is it your business, you idiot? Shoot him now or I'll cancel the contract."

A strange feeling invaded me. I directed my rifle towards the woman.

"My rifle is pointing at you, my dear," I said coldly.

"Whaaat?"

Through my telescope I saw her face, startled, look up in my direction.

"Tell me," I said again, "what did he do wrong?"

"Shoot him now, you fool, or you'll die."

"Actually, it is you who's going to die soon."

"Nonsense! You don't know where I am."

"You're wearing a cheong-sam with a split to the thigh. You're in back of the orchestra."

And I watched her face turn pale.

"You have violated the contract."

"I don't want to shoot innocent people."

"That's none of your business. Last year you shot thousands of innocent people."

"That's my business. Quick, tell me what he did!"

The woman looked like she was going to run.

"Don't run; it's no use. No one will know who shot you. This rifle has a silencer. You know I never miss and I can just disappear."

She looked up in my direction. I could see her cold sweat. Fear.

"What do you want?"

"Tell me what he did."

"He's a traitor. He slandered the name of our country abroad."

"That's all?"

"He slandered people with false statements."

"Then?"

"What do you want? I don't know much."

"I want to know if that is sufficient reason to kill him?"

"That's none of your business. This is politics."

"My business is your pretty pendant. My bullet could shatter it into pieces and it wouldn't stop there."

She looked at me again, beseeching me.

"Don't shoot me! I don't know anything!"

"Who ordered you?"

"I don't know anything."

"Your pretty pendant…"

"Oh, don't, don't shoot! Please…"

"Who?"

"I… I could get into trouble."

"You're in trouble right now. I'll count to three. One…"

"You're crazy! You're ruining everything!"

"Two…" Hmmm… she certainly was nervous.

"He's in front of the person you're supposed to shoot."

"Wearing glasses?"

"Yes."

I directed my rifle there and spotted him. He was talking up a storm. His hands were moving here and there, clenching a fist and striking his other palm with it. His face was cagey and full of deceit. Completely disgusting. In addition to that, he was old.

I aimed the crosshairs of my telescope at his heart while the singer's voice, starting another keroncong melody, echoed in my ear. The music of old people. This would indeed remind them of their past.

this is a keroncong fantasy…

The Sound of Rain on the Roof

"Tell me about fear," said Alina to the storyteller. So the storyteller told her about Sawitri:

Whenever the rain subsided, a tattooed corpse would lie sprawled at the entrance to the alley. That is why Sawitri would tremble whenever she heard the rain start to hit the roof tiles.

Indeed, her house was situated at the corner of the alley's entrance. Sometimes at night she would hear some kind of explosion and the sound of a car in the distance. But often she didn't hear anything, even though a tattooed body would be lying sprawled at the alley's entrance when the rain subsided at night. Perhaps she didn't hear anything because the sound of the rain was so loud. Heavy rain, you know, is often frightening. Even more so if the house is not sturdy, if it has lots of leaks, if it can be flooded, and if it would be crushed if a medium-sized tree fell on it.

Perhaps Sawitri didn't hear anything because she was sleepy and sometimes fell asleep. Perhaps because she turned the radio on too loud. She liked to listen to Indonesian pop music while she was sewing. Often her eyes would sting from looking at the sewing needle hole in 15-watt light. If her eyes began to sting and water, she would close them for a moment. It was when she closed her eyes that she'd listen to the songs on the radio. And when she listened to the songs sometimes she fell sleep. But always, whenever the rain subsided, a tattooed corpse would be lying there sprawled out at the entrance to the alley.

To see the body, Sawitri just had to open the window on the side of her house and look over to the right. She had to bend forward if she wanted to see it clearly. If she didn't then the window shutters would obstruct her view. She had to lean over, pressing her stomach against the window ledge, and then her hair and part of her face would get sprinkled by the last drops of rain.

Her chest would tighten and her heart pound heavily whenever the rain stopped. The sounds of the last raindrops were like the end of a song. But Sawitri would always open the window, lean over and look to the right to see the body. Even though she fell asleep, if it rained in the middle of the night and the rhythm of the rain enticed everyone to forget the transitory world, Sawitri would always wake up when the rain stopped and she would immediately open the window, lean over and look to the right.

She was always afraid, but she always wanted to see the tattooed corpse's face. If her neighbors were crowded around the body, Sawitri would always go outside and squeeze through the crowd until she could see it. She wasn't always able to see the face because sometimes the corpse had already been covered with a cloth, but Sawitri would feel relieved enough when she saw a part of the body, whether it was a foot, a hand, or at least the tattoo.

Once, Sawitri lifted the cloth covering the body to look at its face, but she didn't want to do that ever again. That time she lifted the cloth, she saw a grimacing face with bulging eyes and bared teeth, staring at her as if it was still alive. It was horrifying.

Actually, Sawitri rarely joined the crowd of neighbors. She was almost always the first person to see the tattooed body when the rain had not yet stopped, so that the mist seemed to be a screen shimmering under the yellowish glow of the mercury lamp. The shape of the human body sprawled out like an animal carcass. Sawitri would glance at it just briefly, but long enough to remember how the blood splattered on the wet pavement and how the body was quickly soaked through—the hair, the moustache and the waistline of the trousers.

Not all the corpses' faces were frightening. Sometimes Sawitri got the impression that the tattooed corpse was like a person fast asleep or smiling. Those tattooed people seemed to be smiling and sound asleep in a hammock in a light rain that appeared to her like a curtain on a theater stage. The dim yellow glow of the mercury lamp sometimes turned the color of the blood on the person's chest and back to black, not red. It was the blood that marked the tattooed bodies and distinguished them from sleeping people.

Occasionally, when Sawitri opened her window, leaned over and looked to the right after the rain subsided, the tattooed body's eyes would be staring straight at her. She often felt that she was looking at them at the precise moment their lives ended. They were still alive when their eyes met. And Sawitri could feel how those eyes in their final seeing moments revealed so much. She held the gazes of those tattooed bodies' eyes so often that she could feel whether the person was still alive or not with just a glance. She could sense whether the 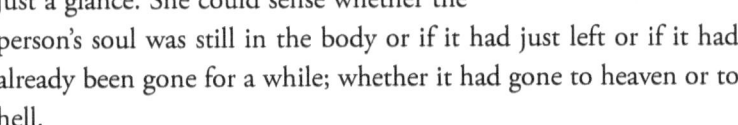 person's soul was still in the body or if it had just left or if it had already been gone for a while; whether it had gone to heaven or to hell.

Sawitri felt as if the eyes told her many stories when she looked at them, but it was difficult to retell those stories. Sometimes she felt the person wanted to scream, that he didn't want to die and still wanted to live, and that he had a wife and children. Occasionally Sawitri saw the eyes asking questions. Eyes demanding their rights. Eyes resisting their fate.

But the stiff tattooed bodies would just get wet. Wet from blood and rain. A flash of lightening made the blood and the wet body shimmer, and the blood and the wet pavement shine. The head hung either to the front or to the back as if forced to accept its own fate. Occasionally, the head turned downward, kissing the earth, or faced upward staring at the sky with wide-open eyes and gaping mouth. And if the rain hadn't really stopped, then Sawitri would see the raindrops splashing into the open mouth.

Sawitri sensed that her neighbors had grown accustomed to the tattooed bodies. In fact, she thought they were happy whenever they saw a tattooed corpse sprawled at the alley's entrance when the rain subsided, highlighted by the yellowish glow of the mercury lamp. From her house at the corner of the alley, she could hear everything they said. They shouted as they crowded around the body, even though sometimes the rain hadn't really stopped. The children would shout, "Hooray, hooray!"

"Look! Another one!"

"Die!"

"Go to hell!"

"Now he knows how it feels!"

"Yeah, now he knows!"

"Dog!"

"Dog!"

Sometimes they would kick the corpse and step on its face. Sometimes they would drag the body by its feet through the neighborhood so that its face would be splattered with mud. Sawitri never joined the happy shouting parade. It was enough to open her window whenever the rain subsided, lean over and look to the right, then close the window again after seeing the shape of the tattooed corpse.

Sawitri would take a deep breath if it turned out that the body was not Pamuji. Didn't Pamuji have a tattoo like those bodies did? And weren't Pamuji's friends amongst the bodies sprawled in the alley's entrance? Occasionally Sawitri knew the tattooed corpses—Kandang Jinongkeng, Pentung Pinanggul…

The bodies were thrown there like rat carcasses tossed into the middle of the street. Sawitri felt that their fate was worse than slaughtered animals. The bodies were thrown down with their hands and feet tied together. Sometimes their hands were tied in back with plastic rope. Sometimes just the thumbs were tied with wire. Sometimes the feet weren't tied. In fact, there were some that weren't tied up at all. But the ones that weren't tied up usually had more bullet wounds. The bullet wounds formed a line across the back or the chest, mutilating the beautiful tattoos.

Sawitri felt that sometimes the shooters of these tattooed bodies had indeed intended to destroy the images. They could have shot only the parts of the body that would cause a fatal wound, but they also shot at places they didn't need to shoot. They also shot at parts of the body that wouldn't kill a person. Did they shoot at those places just to make the tattooed men suffer? Sometimes the tattoos were obliterated by the bullets.

Whenever the rain subsided, she always looked at the tattoo of the person sprawled at the alley's entrance. That was how she

recognized Kandang Jinongkeng. He was lying face down, but
the glow of the mercury lamp was clear enough so that Sawitri
could see the tattoo on his back, which was sprayed   with
bullet holes. The words, I LOVE MAMA, and
a cross on his left arm. Sawitri could remember
clearly the pictures on the bodies. An anchor,
a heart, a rose, a skull, names of women,
sayings, large letters....

Sawitri always paid attention to
the tattoos because Pamuji also had
a tattoo. He had her name tattooed
across his chest. She had written on
his chest, "Sawitri." The name was
enclosed in a heart symbolizing love.
Sawitri remembered that it took her two days to prick Pamuji's
skin with the needle.

But Sawitri's name was not the only tattoo on Pamuji's chest.
She always remembered there was a beautiful rose on his left arm.
Under the rose was written the name, *Nungki*. He said that she was
his first love. Then, there was a picture of a naked woman. On the
naked woman's chest was the name, Asih. According to Pamuji,
he had fallen in love with Asih, but it didn't last. Sawitri knew
Asih. They had both been prostitutes at Mangga Besar. Sawitri met
Pamuji through Asih. Ah, that was all in the past!

The falling rain was like a bad dream. In recent years, ever
since the tattooed bodies began to appear sprawled out at every
corner, life had become a nightmare for Sawitri. Pamuji had
disappeared without a trace.

At first, the bodies were thrown out on to the streets at any
time. Morning, noon, evening, night. Bodies strewn in the corners
of the market, floating in the rivers, buried in the gutters, or

splayed out on the highways. Every day, the newspapers would print photos of tattooed corpses with gun wounds in the neck, forehead, heart, or between the eyes. Occasionally, a tattooed body would be thrown onto the main street in the middle of the day from a car that quickly vanished. The bodies that fell into the middle of a crowd caused a big commotion. People would surround the body yelling, causing a traffic jam. Sawitri saw it once with her own eyes one day while she was shopping. She saw the dust billowing up from the corpse being kicked around. The dust clogged her breath. Pamuji, oh Pamuji, where are you?

The photos of the bodies disappeared from the newspapers, but tattooed corpses with similar traits continued to appear. Their hands and feet were tied. They had been shot fatally, but had bullet wounds in other parts of their bodies. If they were shot in those other places first, they must have really suffered, thought Sawitri. What's more with their hands and feet tied up like that.

Was Pamuji sprawled out somewhere like the bodies at the alley entrance? Once, just once, Sawitri had received a letter from Pamuji without a return address. She was sure he hadn't been caught. Pamuji was very clever. And if the shooters gave him a chance to resist, it wasn't certain that he would lose. Sawitri knew that Pamuji was also a very clever fighter. But, if there was a body sprawled at the alley's end when the rain stopped, who could guarantee that Pamuji had escaped a similar fate?

That is why Sawitri always trembled every time the rain began to drip on the roof tiles. Whenever the rain stopped, a tattooed corpse would lie sprawled at the alley's entrance. Their eyes would always look towards Sawitri as if they knew she was going to open her window and look to the right....

"Will Sawitri meet Pamuji again at the end of the story?" Alina asked the storyteller.

The storyteller answered, "I cannot tell you, Alina. The story has not ended yet."

Grrrh!

Detective Sarman was still sipping, savoring his coffee in Markonah's food stall when his handphone started ringing incessantly. It was late at night. The last drops of a light shower sprinkled down reflecting the glow of the kerosene lantern.

"Officer Sarman?"

"Yes, sir!"

"Go quickly to First Street! There's a riot there!"

"Yes, sir!"

His coffee was still steaming, but Detective Sarman hurried off. He had to let go of his momentary pleasure in the food stall. He had to put aside for a while Markonah's smile, which had long seeped into his heart. Well, such was life, thought Detective Sarman. Chased by events from moment to moment. Whenever he surfaced for a breath, he'd soon be swallowed up by another problem. In the mini-bus heading to the crime site, he felt for his pistol under his jacket. It was still there.

He jumped lightly out of the mini-bus without paying the fare. A crowd had gathered at the side of the road. Detective Sarman's head stood out above the crowd. His eyes quickly recorded a frightening scene.

A figure stood in the moonlight in the middle of the intersection. Occasionally its head would tilt up and out of its mouth an eerie, rough sound would emerge. *Grrrrh! Grrrrh!* No one dared approach it. The figure seemed to be holding a golden necklace that glittered when struck by the light of the street lamps.

Detective Sarman pushed his way forward. Now it was even clearer how frightening the figure was. It was towering and massive, and it was stepping on a victim that was already half dead.

Grrrh! It growled again. And Detective Sarman saw how thick spittle spurt forth from its mouth. Its lips seemed stuck together and only with great force could it open its mouth. Half of its face was decomposing. Its left eye socket was empty and maggots crept out of the socket. *Creech, creech.* The entire body was decaying and the stench was overwhelmingly putrid. Detective Sarman was accustomed to seeing corpses—from victims of accidents to those of torture. Those corpses were often horrifying, but none of them made his hair stand on end.

Here, Detective Sarman saw something he had never seen in his entire life. Maggots were crawling out of holes in the decaying figure. Whenever the maggots fell and crept, *creech, creech,* in the street, more maggots would emerge from the decomposing body and fall, *creech, creech,* followed by more, again and again. *Grrrrh!*

The figure moved as if it was threatening the victim it was standing on. Detective Sarman acted quickly. He took out his pistol. He aimed at the figure's head. He shot.

There was an explosion. The figure was startled. But it didn't stop moving. Detective Sarman's bullet had penetrated its forehead, but no blood flowed forth from the hole. Instead, as if the bullet had punctured a banana tree trunk, maggots crept out of the hole and dropped to the asphalt, *creeech, creeeech.*

Detective Sarman aimed and shot several more times, but the bullets only created more holes. More maggots emerged from every hole, *creech, creech,* making the figure increasingly hideous. It began to move towards Detective Sarman. Its steps were slow, but steady.

Stiff, but sure. Both arms were raised, waving heavily. The crowd scattered. Detective Sarman quickly reached for his handphone.

"Missile! Missile! Send a missile immediately!"

"What for?"

"To shoot the monster! Quick! A 22-caliber isn't enough! Quick! The monster is chasing me! Quick!"

"Monster? What monster?"

"Enough! I'll tell you later! Quick!"

"What kind of missile do you want?"

"Idiot! An anti-tank missile!"

Since the streets were empty, the TOW missile arrived swiftly. The decaying figure was still at a distance from Detective Sarman and it lumbered forward with heavy steps. It would soon be smashed to smithereens. In the blink of an eye, the forty-pound missile was released. The rotting figure was completely destroyed. Only maggots, increasingly more, *creech, creech*, everywhere. *Creech, creech, creech.*

A reporter who had been silently photographing the event quickly hailed a taxi.

"To Palmerah! Quickly!"

The story in the morning newspaper described a nightmare: "Living Corpses Wandering in Capital City." A piece of the news story:

… and our reporters in several corners of the capital city report that living corpses have appeared in every busy area. The bodies were badly decayed. Pistol and rifle bullets were not effective against the decomposing bodies. Even weapons that were enhanced with sorcerers' spells were useless. The living corpses were destroyed only by missiles. But even the missile strikes did not kill them. Pieces of flesh still writhed around and maggots fell from corpses and multiplied in terrifying proportions.

In general, our reporters recorded similar occurrences at all
of the sites. The living corpses, or zombies, act like criminals.
They stole wallets, grabbed necklaces, demanded money,
and committed robbery. However, because their bodies were
decaying, their movements were slow; they could not escape
like criminals. They just waved their plunder in the air while
producing a raspy sound: Grrh! Grrh! They emerged, seemingly
from nowhere. Perhaps directly from the graveyard. However,
there have not yet been any reports of open graves.

"
Doctors are now examining the pieces of flesh that continue
to wriggle. We hope that the government will be able to overcome
these truly strange events. Indeed, in daily life, in this country,
too many illogical matters are blindly accepted. But this matter,
we hope, will be overcome quickly. Living corpses that roam the
streets are too terrifying for reality.

Detective Sarman read the news while shaking his head. "This is
unbelievable! How can it be that my name isn't mentioned? The
press these days always plays up issues that aren't important while
covering up the real issues. Look, where does it mention the hard
working officers? I've been working night and day without rest.
Hey, the living corpse's photo is printed here. Wouldn't be so bad
if it was handsome! People are a pain, too, for always insulting
the police. They only praise the police in Western films. Damn
them!"

He rattled on as he sat in Markonah's food stall eating a piece
of *tempe*.

"Now the newspapers are doing the same thing. News of the
living corpses is everywhere. The community is scared. Later, they'll
blame the police. The police again! The head directs the moves, and
the tail—us—are the ones who'll get hit again. Our monthly salary
covers only a week of living. Damn! If only I had passed the college

entrance exams maybe my fate would have been a little bit better. What do reporters know? Know-it-alls!"

He was still swearing when his handphone rang again. He leaped up.

"Yes, sir!"

Immediately, Detective Sarman took off.

"Hey, where's the money?" shouted Markonah. But she complained only momentarily. She knew Detective Sarman would return. Even though he was married and had four children, he would always come back to her.

Once again, Detective Sarman was facing a living corpse. It was bald, decaying and swarmed by flies. It stood in the intersection with both arms raised. Its mouth was decomposing, but still producing the raspy sound: *Grrh! Grrh!* The streets were jammed. People were abandoning their cars. The decaying figure stomped on the tops of the cars. It slipped occasionally because the soles of its feet were decomposing.

Detective Sarman watched calmly. He knew that even if this one could be disposed of, others would soon emerge. Surely, there was a reason why these rotting bodies were rising up from the netherworld. Surely, there was a reason. If there wasn't, then why were they stirring up trouble?

Maybe, he thought, they had been criminals when they were alive. They could have been rough petty criminals; criminals that had used weapons and physical brawn, but not brains. Detective Sarman noticed that there were traces of tattoos on the decomposing skin. And there were always holes in the bodies from where maggots crawled out and dispersed, *creech creech*. Detective Sarman was on the verge of recalling something, but then lost track of it.

Grrh! That sound yanked him away from his reflections. He focused on the figure again. This one also had tattoos. A vague form of a naked woman could still be detected on its chest. And holes. Yes, the holes were always in the same places. The back of the head, the left side of the chest or forehead. There were some with a line of holes running from the chest to the stomach. Or down the length of the back. But not much else. Again, Detective Sarman seemed to recall something. Again, he heard the sound. *Grrrh!*

He had already ordered the TOW missile—the most efficient weapon to destroy the zombie. He lighted a cigarette as he waited, watching the monster stumble and get up again, slipping on the car tops. It was, indeed, disgusting. The decaying stench reached the spot where Detective Sarman stood. Oh, God! How could a corpse revive? What kind of devil possessed it?

According to the tally, more than twenty living corpses had emerged in various corners of the city. Detective Sarman's friends almost died monitoring them. A TOW missile had been used to destroy each corpse. The unfortunate thing was that the TOW missile did not just annihilate the living corpse, but everything around it as well. The Minister of Environmental Protection was furious.

"Why do they have to use missiles? Isn't it a pity to squander these expensive missiles? Couldn't the zombies be caught in nets? Cut down with machetes? Or showered with gasoline?" questioned a television reporter.

In the meantime, a controversy evolved. The living corpses were emerging everywhere. The officials wanted to dispose of them quickly, and for this, missiles were indeed the most effective means.

However, so many corpses had appeared in just a few days. Detective Sarman wondered what would happen if they ran out of missiles. His brain spun. The United States was not selling missiles at the time. To buy them from Israel would be an act of betrayal. There had to be another way. Who knew how many more living corpses would emerge to terrorize us? Where did these decaying corpses come from? Detective Sarman was truly perplexed. He reached for his handphone.

"Examine all the cemeteries in every corner of the country. Report back which graves are open!" ordered Detective Sarman.

The missile arrived at that moment. The officers carried it carefully. The zombie stood erect on the top of a car. *Grrh! Grrrh!* Detective Sarman examined the decomposing face. It seemed familiar. Who was it? *Grrh! Grrh!* Maggots oozed out of its mouth. And, as usual, it moved hideously, *creech, creech*. The maggots multiplied rapidly, creeping on to the car windows causing the pretty women passengers who hadn't run away to scream hysterically. The zombie seemed to become more ferocious.

"Quick, shoot!" screamed Detective Sarman.

"Okay, boss!"

The TOW missile was quickly released. *Sssrrrrrrr!*

It was as if the capital city was swept up in a war. In the aftermath of the missile strike, there was rubble and debris scattered everywhere. But the zombies kept emerging. The maggots squirmed out of them like an infestation. The maggots crept, *creech, creech*, on tables, chairs, windows; in restrooms, bathrooms, shirt pockets, shoes, plates, glasses, and bottles. Every day people were busy flicking off maggots that had crept on to their clothes, hair, nostrils, or hung off their eyeglasses.

The zombies were everywhere. Chaos reigned. They not only seized cheap objects, but also started to devour all kinds of food. Their presence spread terror. The government was running out of missiles, which was understandable because the country was usually peaceful and quiet, fertile and prosperous. Damn! Who would have dreamed that they would have to fight zombies?

Detective Sarman's handphone rang.

"Officer Sarman?"

"Yes, sir!"

"Quickly, go to Fifth Street! There's another zombie!"

"Yes, sir!"

But Detective Sarman did not move. He put his feet on the desk in the office. His head hung limply. The handphone kept ringing. The conversation went in circles.

He lazily reached for several reports that had been submitted.

... informants from all corners of the country report that a number of graves have been excavated. The caskets have been opened and lie empty. These opened graves are the graves of third-class criminals. However, not all graves bear names or years. This investigation also indicates that some of the living corpses originated from the Big Hole ...

This reminded Detective Sarman of something. Before he could determine the answer, there was a knock on the window behind him. He turned and stopped short. It was a zombie!

His heart pounded. A decomposing face suddenly appeared in the window. In that instant, although the face was decaying, Detective Sarman recognized it.

"Ngadul!" he screamed. But Ngadul, the zombie, did not recognize him anymore. The zombie slithered into his office. *Grrrh! Grrrh!*

Detective Sarman leapt up on to the desk and reached for his handphone. He realized something.

"Commander! One of the zombies is Ngadul! One of the victims of that infamous controversial slaughter at Big Hole! I recognize him, sir! He's here at the headquarters!"

"Quickly, shoot him with a missile."

"I'm sorry, Commander! That will not solve the problem!"

The zombie advanced towards Sarman's desk and turned it over. The officer quickly jumped off and ran into another room. The zombie followed him. Maggots crept up the walls.

"Officer Sarman! Are you refusing to carry out your commander's order?"

"No, sir! We don't have enough missiles to annihilate all of the zombies."

"What do you mean, Officer Sarman? The zombies are creating havoc!"

The zombie kicked the door down. Detective Sarman leapt to the window.

"Don't you remember? Along with Ngadul, six thousand third-class criminals were secretly wiped out! Do you remember, sir?"

"Yes, yes! Why?"

"Most of the corpses were buried at the Big Hole, Commander, sir."

"I know. So what?"

"There's a report—many of them had retired from crime, sir! Many of those who were mysteriously butchered down had already reformed, sir! And no prayers were recited for them. At that time no one dared! They were afraid of being butchered too, sir, because at that time just anyone could be killed mysteriously, sir!"

Grrh! The zombie leapt from the window. Detective Sarman scaled the courtyard walls.

"So, what is your conclusion, Officer Sarman?"

"The slaughter was a big mistake, sir! Our generation is suffering the consequences! Those people weren't willing to die, sir! They're taking their revenge!"

"What do we have to do?"

"Pray for them, sir! We have to hold a mass prayer, sir! We have only one hundred missiles! That's not enough to destroy them! Pray for them, sir, so their souls will rest in peace!"

"Are you dreaming, Officer Sarman? You're talking in your sleep! That's all nonsense! We're importing missiles from abroad right now! Do you hear that? Six thousand missiles are being shipped here! The corpses will be destroyed!"

The zombie caught Detective Sarman's leg, which was still on the courtyard side of the wall.

"Help! It caught me! Help!"

Detective Sarman screamed hysterically. The zombie started to bite his leg. Sarman's screams reached the heavens. His handphone fell into the gutters.

Zombies appeared in several corners of the city, more and more, faster and faster, wilder and wilder. They crept like maggots. Filling the streets, creeping into supermarkets, entering campuses. They wandered into all remote corners. Scaling high-rise buildings and screeching hoarsely. *Grrrh! Grrh!* Revenge! Revenge! They spoke together like a chorus from hell. *Grrh! Grrrh!* Revenge! Retaliate! *Grrrh!*

Detective Sarman's shrill cry sliced through the terrifying chorus that caused the entire city to tremble with fear: "Help! My leg is being eaten by a zombie! *Help! Commander! Help!*"

II.
Stories for Alina

Sarman

"Tell me about boredom," said Alina to the storyteller. So the storyteller told her the story about Sarman:

One clear day, on payday, Sarman caused a stir. After receiving his envelope filled with his wages plus additional subsidies, and after signing for it, Sarman mused. But only briefly. He then screamed in a loud voice, "So this is what I work for every day, is it? For this lousy stack of paper?!"

He stood up; his face was tense. He held the envelope in his left fist; his right hand pointed at the envelope. His eyes, burning with rage, glared at the envelope.

"You bastard! You wretch! You fiend! You devil! Despicable! I refuse to be enslaved to you! I renounce you!"

The office, which was usually busy, cool, and indifferent, with soft music playing in the background, suddenly erupted into a commotion.

"Hey, what's up, 'Man? Why are you angry so early in the morning?"

"Say, Sarman, what is it?"

"I hope it's not because he hasn't eaten yet."

"Maybe he's possessed."

"'Man! Sarman! Cool down, 'Man! You'll get called in!"

But Sarman didn't stop. He jumped onto the table. He tore open the brown envelope and grabbed the money. He ripped the paper binding off the bundle and threw some of the money into the air.

"Here! Eat it! As of today, I don't need to be paid! Do you hear that?! I don't need to be paid! I'll work for free, just as hard as usual! Do you monkeys hear that?!"

Dozens of ten thousand rupiah notes blown by the air conditioning unit floated in the air. The office flew into disarray. Without shame, the office workers scrambled and grabbed for Sarman's money. Men and women crowded, shoved, pushed, and vaulted over each other, grasping for the fortune floating in the air. They quickly stuffed the money into their pockets then pretended not to notice anything.

Sarman kicked all the objects off his desk—folders piled up in a stack, typewriter, a glass of tea, even the photo of his family. Even the computer monitor screen was thrashed.

"Sarman! You're crazy!"

Sarman leapt from table to table like a fighter in a martial arts movie. He kicked objects on the other workers' desks, swearing the entire time. It wasn't clear what he was swearing at.

In a short time, the seventeenth floor office was a mess. The secretaries were screaming, "Aaaaa!" and the male employees, revealing their cowardliness, didn't dare to do anything, even though they were hoping that Sarman would throw away the rest of the money he was holding.

Sarman was not unaware of this.

"You want this money? Huh? You want this money? Sukab! You want money? Here! You want money? Here! You all want this money? Here! Here! Here! Eat it!"

Sarman threw the money to his friends while leaping from table to table. The office workers became insects that followed Sarman around wherever he went. The office dissolved into chaos.

The workers were like ravenous cats. They grabbed greedily. Those who jumped were pushed and fell. Those who lunged at the money on the floor had their feet pulled out from under them. More than a little money was torn in the tussle. Pulling, scratching, kicking blindly.

"Hey, do you still want more money?" Sarman asked, standing on the boss' desk.

They answered in unison. "Yeeesssss!"

Sarman smiled. Sweat dripped from his forehead. He loosened his tie that was strangling him.

"Okay! But you have to yell, 'Long live money! Long live money!' Agreed?"

"Agreeeeed!"

So, like a softball player pitching a ball, Sarman threw out another fistful of bills. The bills scattered in the air, dancing like fake snowflakes on a stage during a Christmas pageant. The office workers' eyes glistened happily, their mouths hung open, their faces reflected their pathetic determination.

"Attaaaaack!" they yelled in unison. The fighting resumed. Now they were wrestling as if in a party game. They broke into giggles. Preoccupied, they were unaware that many buttons had fallen off, shoes loosened, dresses wrinkled, and hair tangled. Sarman squatted like a young child. He leapt from table to table, turning somersaults. The room resounded with yells. Although they were not in unison since they were screaming while grabbing for money in the air and under the tables: Long live money! Long live money!

Suddenly, the section supervisor appeared. He stood quietly in the doorway watching the chaotic scene. His face was frozen in authority. Then he strode toward his desk as if nothing was happening.

Initially, the workers didn't realize he was there and they continued to laugh while they lunged for the money. Those who noticed his presence calmed down quickly, returned to their desks, and pretended to work even though their desks were a mess, having been trashed by Sarman.

Gradually everyone realized the section supervisor was there. They retreated quickly. They held money in both hands. The rest of it still lay scattered on the floor, chairs, tables, wastebaskets, mixed with spilled coffee and broken glass. Papers were strewn in disarray, as in the saying "like a shipwreck."

Sarman remained standing on a desk. His hair was tousled, his face wild like a cornered animal, his usually neat clothes and shiny shoes were now rumpled and scuffed. The section supervisor almost didn't recognize Sarman, his most diligent worker who had climbed the professional ladder quickly.

"Try to explain. What is the meaning of all this?" he asked patiently, but firmly.

Everyone was quiet. Their eyes were fixed on Sarman, who was still panting heavily, standing above them on the desk. In the silence, the soft background music could be heard again, but it didn't lighten the atmosphere.

The section supervisor's attention finally turned to Sarman.

"Sarman, can you come down from the desk?" he asked.

"I can, sir, but I don't want to."

"Why not?"

"It's a very long answer, sir. I don't need to explain."

"Why not? We can talk about it in another room and—"

"No sir! Don't try to persuade me!" Sarman shouted. "Today, I refuse my pay, refuse to work, refuse to follow your orders. I refuse whatever should happen. I don't like this situation. I hate it!"

The section supervisor approached him. With a fatherly look, he tried to calm down his favorite employee.

"Do you need a vacation, Sarman? You can take a long leave of absence, a one-month vacation. You've worked here for ten years."

But Sarman stamped on the desk, kicking the remaining stacks of paper on the desk, then jumping again to another one. The woman sitting there was frozen with fear. She didn't dare move.

"Don't come any closer! I already explained that as of today, I refuse everything! Understand? I refuse whatever any of you want!"

The section supervisor wanted to be angry and throw Sarman out, but he was too important to the company. Moreover, it just wasn't right to fire an employee who had served as well as Sarman had. Meanwhile, the employees from the other sections began to gather. News of the incident spread quickly. Several security officers entered the room. They were about to move into action, but the section supervisor restrained them.

"Wait! Let me handle this! I know him. Sarman has been my employee for years."

So the security officers busied themselves with their handphones. A telephone ringing on one of the desks broke the silence, but Sarman quickly jumped over to it and kicked it. He was still holding a fistful of money. His salary was, indeed, one of the highest in the office, which was understandable, as he had worked there for ten years.

"Why are you doing this, Sarman? Why?" asked the section supervisor.

"That is not at all important!"

"Then, what do you want? You can take a long vacation starting today. You can claim the subsidies today. You can use the company's hotel in Bali or the company's villa at Puncak. Just go. We'll finish your work. Frankly, all this time we've been too—"

"What? Vacation? Did you say 'vacation?!'" Sarman exclaimed, cupping his hand to his ear. "A long vacation after ten years of work? A vacation? Ha ha ha ha! A vacation? Ha ha ha ha! A long vacation and then work again for ten more years? Ha ha ha! Ha ha ha! You can take your vacation, sir!"

Then Sarman made a karate lunge for the window. The thick seventeenth-story window did not shatter easily. Sarman punched it several times until his hand bled. He hurled a chair at the window and only then did it shatter. A fierce wind swept through the office. Papers flew around. Sarman leapt to the window. He was ready to jump. This caused another commotion and everyone screamed.

"Sarman! Don't jump, Sarman!"

"Don't throw your life away, Sarman! Think of your children and your wife! Think of your parents in the village! Think of your friends!"

"Sarman! Use your head! Use your good sense! Your life has meaning! Your life is not useless!"

Sarman, who had been facing the highway outside, turned around, kicking at the shards of glass left on the window frame. He screamed furiously.

"Damn all of you! Damn you! For ten years, I woke up every morning and rushed to this office! For ten years, I put my attendance card in that cursed machine every morning and evening! For ten years, I worked at the same job for eight hours a day! For ten years! And I will for many more years! Of course, I was paid for it and the pay was not insufficient! But it was all just nonsense! A vacation is nonsense too! This isn't your fault! And it's not the company's fault! It's all just a bunch of nonsense! Do you get it, you monkeys? This is all just nonsense!"

"Sarman's gone crazy," whispered someone.

"What happened to him?" someone else whispered.

"This is just temporary; it'll be swept away like dust!"

Sarman continued to rant on.

"Do you still remember the numbers you wrote down yesterday? Do you still remember the sentences you wrote yesterday?

Do you still remember the names on our client list yesterday? Do you still remember the numbers of our new office cars? Do you still remember the names of our friends who have left this company? Do you still remember the bums who always give us commissions? So many, so close, but how meaningless. We are all trash! I am just trash! So, enough, don't go to any trouble! You'll forget all about this tomorrow! Vanished, vaporized, swept away like dust! Like trash in the corner of the warehouse! Like oil on the workshop floor! Like screws..."

While Sarman was making his speech, the security officers had an idea. They called the fire department. But their arrival caused a commotion.

"Where's the fire, sir?"

"It's not a fire!"

"What is it?"

"Someone's going to commit suicide."

"Where?"

"There!"

So it was, there on the seventeenth floor, the people on the street could see that a window was gaping open. Sarman could be seen. His figure was tiny, but clear; facing inside and screaming. The people below stopped to look up. Cars stopped. Traffic jammed. Suddenly, Sarman had become a spectacle. Several people used binoculars; some people took photos with telephoto lens. The firemen spread out the safety net. The fire truck ladder, which reached only 40.9 meters high, stretched upward. The hoses, which could pump volumes of water upward and help to reduce the velocity of Sarman's falling body should he jump, were prepared. Traffic was totally jammed. A police helicopter hovered in the vicinity. Observers sat on car roofs. Several people placed bets of considerable sums on whether Sarman would commit suicide or not. The television news crew arrived late.

Another step to stop Sarman was taken. Sarman's wife and youngest child were in the police helicopter.

"Sarman, look, there's your child and your wife!" the workers in the building screamed.

"Yeah, it's your wife and child! Think about them, Sarman! Don't be rash!"

"Sarman! Sarman! It's me, your wife, Sarman! I love you! The children love you too! Don't jump, Sarman!" bawled his wife. Her voice reverberated through the loudspeaker, resonating over the drone of the helicopter.

"Daddy! Daddy!" shouted his child.

Sarman turned around. The woman waved frantically while tears streamed down her cheeks. His heart stopped. He wanted to wave back, like he always did every morning when he left for the office, but this reminded him of the fistful of money still in his hand. Sarman relapsed. Inside the office two security officers were edging slowly towards the window.

"Think of our children, Sarman! They need you! Think of your mother—she's coming from the village this week! Sarman, oh Sarman, don't leave me!" his wife screamed again.

"What?! Go home to you?! To face all of your trifles?! Go home to face all your nonsense?! You never know how I feel! You only care about my obligations! You only care about this!"

Sarman held up the money in his hand.

"You only know about this, right?"

"That's not true! Sarman, I didn't mean that! You misunderstand me, Sarman. I—"

"This is your money! Eat it!"

And Sarman threw hundreds of thousands of rupiah into the air. The money in his hand was gone. The bills floated in the wind, twisting and glistening in the sun's rays.

"Sarman, oh, Sarman…" his wife sobbed.

His child screamed, "Daddy! Daddy!"

The wind blew briskly at this height. Sarman watched his money float down. It hadn't reached the ground yet. Still floating, scattering. People in offices below Sarman's were surprised to see money floating in the air. Children and adults below were preparing to catch it. The atmosphere turned merry. Sarman mused. This play could end in a flash.

At that moment, two security guards crept towards the window. One of them lunged forward to grab Sarman, but this movement, a movement that the guard had executed for the first time in his life, was not perfect. Sarman dodged him by reflex and slipped. The guard desperately caught only Sarman's shoe.

The people below screamed hysterically. Those inside the building fought for a view from one of the windows. Sarman's body plummeted down. He had a chance to reflect—the play was now reality. With dance-like movements, Sarman's body shot past the bills that had not yet reached the ground. The firefighters spread the safety net as widely as possible below. Four water hoses shot water up in his direction.

"Will Sarman be saved?" Alina asked anxiously.

"Oh, that is not important at all, Alina," answered the storyteller. "It's not at all important."

The Last *Becak* in the World (or Rambo)

"Tell me about extinction," said Alina to the storyteller. So the storyteller told her the story about Rambo:

The sky was tinged with lavender. Evening swallowed the city. A convoy of hundreds of trucks streamed across the desert, carrying thousands of *becak* carts. Dust billowed up behind the black shadow that strung out like a giant serpent. The seemingly endless chain of trucks carrying thousands of becaks snaked out of the city. Thunderous music echoed in the drivers' ears. Hundreds of truck drivers using Walkman tape recorders. Hundreds of Walkmans reverberating desert music.

Hundreds of trucks speeding through the desert. Becaks riding in the truck beds, their wheels revolving and joggling. The dust clouds billowing back. From a distance, the clouds seemed to be rising from the sunset's last rays. Hundreds of trucks shooting forward without turning. Thousands of people squatted along the edge of the truck line, eyes empty. Their arms hanging hopelessly. Occasionally, someone would utter a weak cry. Heedlessly, the drivers pressed on the gas pedals. Their eyes locked forward. They didn't glance either left or right. Their ears echoed with thundering desert music. Deafening.

Hundreds of trucks rumbled towards the beach. The waves pounded against the shore as if the god of the sea was famished.

Hundreds of trucks reached the beach. The waves crashed and the wind howled. Hundreds of trucks lined up side-by-side with their backs to the sea. Hundreds of truck beds were raised at the same time and thousands of becaks were poured into hundreds of cargo boats. Hundreds of cargo boats carried thousands of becaks over the wild waves. Hundreds of cargo boats dumped thousands of becaks into the middle of the sea at the same time. Thousands of becaks sank to the bottom of the ocean dispersing the fishes. Those becaks would become wrecks soon.

A man stood erect, watching the scene from the edge of a cliff. With the evening sky in the background he appeared as only a black shadow. He stood as still as a statue, his eyes focused sharply on the hundreds of boats throwing out thousands of becaks. He stayed there until the boats returned to the beach and the trucks headed back to the city, leaving a long trail of dust. A becak was visible beside the man's black shadow.

At nightfall, he steered his becak down the hill. At the bottom of the hill, a woman waved her hand: "'Cak!"

The becak stopped.

"How much to the market, brother?"

"Five hundred."

"How about two hundred?"

"Get in."

The becak sped through the desert heading for the shimmering city. They passed the thousands of people who had been squatting along the road staring with empty eyes.

"Rambo!" they screamed when they saw the becak.

"What?!"

"Be careful, Rambo!"

"Why?"

"Watch out! Your becak is the last becak in the world!"

"I know."

Yes. It was Rambo, the becak driver. He was very well built. He was handsome, though a bit stupid-looking. He pedaled his becak furiously. The wind played with his long hair. The ends of his headcloth waved. One could hear faintly, coming down from the sky, the song:

My brave strong horse is running ...

Indeed, this was not just any ordinary becak driver. Nor was the becak he pedaled just any ordinary becak. It was the Golden Becak. Rambo had won the Great Paris-to-Dakar Race in the becak class with that becak. He had circled the world three times with that becak. He had been in a traveling circus that featured becak attractions. Rambo could maneuver the becak on a rope—the one back wheel on the rope with the two front wheels lifted up in the air. And that was not all that he could do with his becak.

The Golden Becak now headed for the city. Sweat poured down Rambo's body. His undershirt was drenched. Even the swimming trunks he was wearing were wet. Occasionally, he wiped his face with the small towel hung around his neck. Wearing basketball shoes, he pedaled without stopping. The woman sat leisurely in the becak. Her legs were crossed and her hands combed through her hair over and over again.

The Golden Becak passed through the city gates with the speed of the wind. The sentries—carrying Armalites and Kalashnikovs and daydreaming—were caught off-guard. One of them quickly shot a volley, but missed.

"That's crazy! There's still a becak in the city!"

"That's the last becak that hasn't been confiscated!"

"Quickly, report it!"

Within minutes, the city dissolved into commotion. Police sirens wailed. Police cars with flashing red lights shot down the streets, searching for the only becak that was still loose.

Rambo squeezed in between the other vehicles. The people in the cars and on the sidewalk who saw him were astounded.

"Look! The Golden Becak hasn't been caught!"

"It's Rambo!"

Rambo's sweat glistened, awash in the glare of the giant neon signs.

"Where's the market?" he shouted over the sounds of the surrounding cars.

"Still far!"

"Where?"

"The end of the world!" And the woman laughed for a long time. But before Rambo could understand what she meant, the sound of a police car siren could be heard approaching. The police car was in front of him intercepting his route. Rambo adeptly turned his becak. He shot down narrow alleys, then emerged onto another main street.

Officers with handphones on every street quickly reported when they spotted the Golden Becak.

"Rambo is on First Street!"

"The Golden Becak is on Second Street!"

Every exit was blocked, but Rambo was still able to deceive them. Sometimes he pedaled his becak to soar over the police cars. Meanwhile, the woman in the becak kept laughing while combing her hair.

Almost the entire police force had been activated. Sirens wailed throughout the streets. Traffic stalled. Rambo was able to maneuver through it acrobatically. He pedaled the Golden Becak furiously in a variety of ways. Sometimes the becak ran on its side on just two wheels, but not infrequently, it also ran on only one wheel. Television cameramen positioned strategically immortalized Rambo's flight.

One television reporter commented:

"This is incredible! No less than three thousand police officers are chasing the last becak in the world! But they haven't caught the Golden Becak driven by Rambo! It looks like Rambo knows more about the city streets than the police do. He races on! He passes! He swerves! Rambo flies like the devil from the end of one street to the end of another. From alley to alley! From bridge to bridge! Look, viewers! You can see it on your television screens! One becak driver chased by three thousand police officers! This is history! You are witnessing the fate of the last becak in the world driven by the best, and the last, becak driver in the world!"

Television viewers were riveted by Rambo's flight. The cameramen were no less agile. They followed Rambo every inch of the way. The reporters took turns covering the chase from their respective vantage points.

"Viewers, wherever you are! Look at Rambo's sweat dripping like pearls! He's panting! His face is calm, but he's simmering with anger! He continues to pedal his becak! He sees clearly! My God! Viewers at home! Look at his eyes! His eyes harbor revenge! Revenge that will never be avenged! There has never been a becak driver with eyes like this! Becak drivers' eyes are usually drained, lazy and resigned! But this? Viewers throughout the country, do Rambo's eyes reflect the feelings of all of the becak drivers in the world whose becaks have been confiscated?"

Rambo continued to pedal his becak. He was able to outdistance the police chase. He entered the slums where the police cars could not pursue him. Actually, a police motorcycle could still chase him if it wanted to, but many of them had been damaged after flipping over while chasing Rambo on the main streets. They had been swept into ditches one by one. Those remaining were too afraid to enter this area. It was understandable as they could be struck in the back by unseen hands. The cameramen were also hesitant to enter the area, keeping in mind that their equipment was expensive. So, they ascended to the tops of tall buildings and aimed their cameras from there.

From that height, it appeared that Rambo had slowed down. People were dancing to *dangdut* rhythms at the end of the street under the glare of a kerosene lantern.

My life is for love
Unrequited love

"I'll get off here. This is the place," the woman said suddenly, continuing to comb her hair.

"Is this the end of the world?"

The woman laughed.

"You can sleep at my place," she said, while pulling Rambo's arm. The becak driver just followed. They disappeared into the darkness.

"They disappeared into the darkness! Viewers at home, Rambo and his female passenger have gone into the shack. From this reporter's vantage point, I can only see the Golden Becak parked in front of a shabby hut usually used by prostitutes. Viewers at home, people are not paying too much attention to Rambo in this shady area. They are also not paying much attention to the three thousand police officers hunting down the Golden Becak. They themselves have too often been arrested and detained. They are…"

The television reporter continued to report on the situation. Meanwhile, one by one, army soldiers appeared around the slum area. They crept forward slowly with M-16 rifles in their hands. Several of them carried bazookas.

Inside the hut, the two people were talking.

"I'm a hooker. I'm always getting arrested. We have the same fate of being condemned."

"But they'll never arrest all the hookers. It's different for becaks. My becak is the last one in the world. There will never be a last prostitute in the world. You are luckier…"

"Ah, that's enough, Rambo," the young hooker said as she wiped the sweat off his face. Then she pulled the becak driver's head to herself and kissed him. They made love.

A thin ray of light shone on the Golden Becak that was sitting outside. Rambo had locked the wheel with a chain and tied it to a pole.

"Viewers throughout the country…" This time the reporter's voice was low, almost a whisper. "One army unit has arrived to ambush Rambo. It's understandable—this is the last becak in this world that hasn't been confiscated, so the authorities are ashamed. Not just ashamed because they aren't able to eradicate becaks, but also ashamed because becaks still exist in this modern country. For this crime, Rambo may receive the death penalty. Indeed, the former becak drivers haven't gotten new jobs yet, but it's far more important that the face of the city is clean and the streets appear more attractive without becaks. Our nation is developing. Television viewers, the situation is increasingly tense. The broken-down shack where Rambo and the woman entered has been tightly surrounded. Strains of dangdut music can be heard faintly. You can see on your screen that the soldiers are creeping forward with weapons in their hands. Nevertheless, the people dancing at the end of the street don't care. Now, look, the operations commander is speaking through a loudspeaker…"

"Rambo! Surrender! You are surrounded! You can't escape! Surrender your becak voluntarily!"

It was quiet. No answer. The night felt calmer.

"If you give up, we'll give you a job! You don't have to pedal a becak!"

Silence. The sound of rats squeaking in the gutters.

"We'll give you a *bajaj!* A Golden Bajaj!

The sound of a woman laughing could be heard coming from inside the shack.

"Hey, how many bajaj are there for all the former becak drivers?" screamed the woman in the midst of a long laugh.

"Damn you, Rambo! We don't have any other choice! We're sorry. Actually, we sympathize with you; we're only doing our job! Prepare to attack! One… two…"

Suddenly, the door of the shabby hut opened.

"Stop! I surrender!" Rambo raised his two hands. His face was drained, lazy, resigned. The hooker shyly followed behind him.

"Oh my God, viewers! Our hero is surrendering! The symbol of our rebellion is giving up! This is truly embarrassing! This can't happen! No! Rambo! Don't give up, Rambo! Die like a soldier! Die like a hero!" The television reporters screamed from the tops of the buildings. In their homes, the television viewers were also yelling wildly. The city was in tumult.

"Don't be shameful, Rambo!"

"Damn you, Rambo!"

"We don't have a symbol anymore!"

"We aren't brave enough ourselves!"

"Rambo! Damn you! How much are you being paid?!"

Many people kicked and threw things at their television screens until they shattered.

"So, are you surrendering, Rambo?" the commander asked. Rambo moved forward with his two hands still raised.

"Yes, I am surrendering. I'm not a hero. And I don't want to be a hero. I'm just a becak driver who is afraid of dying and needs to eat…"

The commander smiled fleetingly, then suddenly shouted, "Fiiire!"

"Stop! Stop! Don't go on!" screamed Alina to the storyteller. "I can imagine what's going to happen! Why did the story have to end that way?"

"The times change, Alina. The dinosaurs became extinct. The Apache tribe became extinct. Becaks too will become extinct...."

"Times change, but why do we have to change, too?"[1]

The storyteller did not answer. He just grinned like a statue of the Laughing Buddha.

---

[1] This question recalls the words of Seiichi (Higashi Igawa) in the film *Kokyo* (Home from the Sea), directed by Yoji Yamada (1972). Upon reexamination, the question in the film was: "People say that times have changed. Why must I also change?" The author of this story viewed this film during Japanese Film Week at Taman Ismail Marzuki in Jakarta in 1977.

The Potted Jasmine Plant

"Tell me about memories," said Alina to the storyteller while offering him a cup of coffee. So the storyteller told her the story about the potted jasmine plant:

Twelve years ago, a husband and wife sat on a narrow veranda, talking about the full moon.

"Look, the moon is so beautiful," said the woman.

"Actually, it's just a moon," her husband replied. "If it weren't for the sun's light, the moon would not be visible."

"But the moon is beautiful. Look."

"It's the sun that makes the moon beautiful."

"That's not important and I don't want to know about that. I only know that the moon is truly beautiful. Imagine if there were no electric lights, the moonbeams would—"

"You must accept reality. There is no full moon without the sun. Beauty is…"

They continued talking while viewing the full moon. Some of the stars, so many light years away, were obscured by wispy clouds surrounding the moon and, especially by the yellow glow of the mercury streetlights in front of their house. Occasionally, the passing glare of the pressure lamps of the omelet, fried noodle and tofu vendors interrupted their pleasure in viewing the full moon. What's more, the voices of children running in the street in front of their house, interspersed with sounds of *bajaj* engines, *becak* bells, or motorcycle horns, produced so much clamor that they couldn't hear each other so they had to repeat themselves.

Despite this annoyance, they continued to converse. Heavy clouds covered the moon. Rain clouds filled the sky. It was humid. They conversed about everything that passed through their minds. The woman, who was almost forty years old, wore jeans and a T-shirt. She sat in a rocking chair dangling her legs and spoke as she sniffed the jasmine blossoms of a potted plant she was holding.

They talked about leaves, about people, and about prices. They talked about barbed wire, an iron trellis, and pop songs. They talked about the past, the future, their goals, and their dreams. They also spoke about their children and their cats and dogs.

Then the rain began to fall and they talked about the rain.

"People say that Jakarta is romantic in the rainy season," the woman said. She was still sniffing the sweet jasmine blossoms and occasionally examined the plant closely.

"During the rainy season Jakarta floods, the streets clog, and then all kinds of plans are messed up. Essentially, it's hell. What's romantic about that?"

"I like rain. I like the smell of damp earth. The asphalt on the streets seems fresh when the rain stops. The streets glisten at night. The colors shimmer. Even the rain on the windows is lovely in the rainy season. I like to drive the car, shooting through the rain. You know, when it rains sometimes I feel lonely, all by myself. The children are never at home. You too, whenever..."

The husband was startled for a second. But his wife continued to talk without looking at him, as if she was speaking to the jasmine flowers in her hands. The man seemed to recall something, but he didn't try to hold on to it.

The next morning, he had already forgotten the conversation of the previous night. The days passed quickly. Events lost their importance. Things came and left without leaving any meaningful impressions. Life became a series of meaningless ceremonies and obligations.

The wife died a year after that conversation.

Later, the man reminisced about his wife. He recalled their conversation about the moon, leaves, barbed wire, pop songs, even about the rainy season. However, the image he remembered the most was his wife sniffing the fragrant jasmine blossoms. The way his wife spoke while gazing carefully at the jasmine plant in her hands was embedded in his memory.

Later, on his day off when he didn't know what to do, he happened to notice the jasmine plant in the pot. The clear morning sun swept across the flowerpots on the narrow veranda. Almost all of the flowerpots were cracked. There were still a few drops of dew on the leaves. Dripping one by one. In the past, on vacation days like this, his wife would always want to go to buy house plants from the street-side plant vendors. They bought potted plants, then arranged them on their narrow veranda.

"In Jakarta, the yards are small, but we must always have space," his wife always said. He had forgotten that sentence, but now it constantly buzzed in his ear. Suddenly, the man realized that they had not bought the potted jasmine plant. He remembered now where they bought the aster, hibiscus, violet rose, and orchid plants that still thrived sweetly, although a bit wildly. He was sure that they never bought the jasmine plant. So, where did it come from?

He called his daughter.

"Where did Mama get this jasmine plant?"

"What, have you forgotten? That's Grandma's jasmine!"

"From Grandma? This jasmine was brought here from Surabaya?"

"Yes, Mama carried it on her lap in the plane. When Papa was still in Bangkok."

"Oh…"

On that day off, he felt as if the past flooded back to him. If he had a video recording that documented everything that had happened when the owner was away, it was now time to play back the recording. He felt emptiness in his heart, but he couldn't avoid it; he couldn't stop thinking about it.

He could envision his wife watering the plants in the little garden.

"Mother took special care of this jasmine plant," his wife said.

"The blossoms from that plant were used for the flower tassel for Nita's hair when she got married, remember?"

"You didn't mention it then."

"Ah, you always forget. You always forget everything I say."

"Oh, really?"

"Yes. A long, long, long, *long* time ago you were different, but now…"

Now, he remembered. He was going to ask whether she had brought that jasmine plant from Surabaya, but a guest arrived just then. He also remembered he wanted to ask why she brought the plant from Surabaya and then took special care of it just as her mother had. But those questions remained unasked. Now, he remembered it all clearly. He asked in his heart how could he remember all those unasked questions after all these years.

He asked his daughter again, "What did Mama say about this jasmine plant?"

"Ah, I forgot, Pa."

"What?! How could you just forget?!"

"Papa, what is this? Do we have to remember everything Mama said about that jasmine plant?"

Her father did not answer. The daughter tried to think of something to satisfy her father, but she couldn't find the right words.

The day passed.

Ever since then, the daughter often saw her father watering her mother's favorite plant. Actually, it was not often because her father was rarely at home, but watering plants was not something her father usually did. Her father also often reminded her to look after her mother's jasmine plant. Sometimes, if the plant was flowering, her father would take a fistful of blossoms and put them in his pocket. Sometimes, when he was relaxing, she saw him daydreaming, sitting in the rocking chair on the narrow veranda. She saw him sniffing the fragrant jasmine blossoms and gazing at them for a long time.

The daughter sensed that her father felt something of her mother in the flowers. Something perhaps that he didn't acknowledge when she was alive, but that was embodied in the jasmine plant.

Ten years later, her father died.

When the inheritance was settled, none of the five children, except for the one daughter whom the father had asked, wanted the mother's plants.

The house was sold. The five children spread out to five corners of the world. After she marryied, the daughter took the jasmine plant to her apartment on the forty-fourth floor of a building in New York. It was the only object of inheritance left. Her four siblings had sold everything they inherited. They sold their rice fields, their land, their house, their jewelry and furniture—they sold everything. In the end, even the *keris* was sold. Their mother's houseplants did not escape as they were sold back to the plant vendors. Except for the jasmine plant. The daughter requested that the jasmine plant not be sold and her siblings agreed because they didn't think it was important.

Her father had never spoken about his feelings for the jasmine plant. Neither had her mother. At the time, she didn't really want to know. Her father never told her that the jasmine plant reminded him about a conversation about the moon, leaves, barbed wire, pop songs, and the rainy season, on a night when her mother spoke while gazing at the jasmine plant in her hands.

Her mother also had never told her that her mother had potted the jasmine plant in Surabaya when her own father died. Her mother didn't tell her that she felt something of her own mother in that plant, and when she went to Surabaya when her mother died, she brought the potted jasmine home to Jakarta.

She never heard those stories, but she felt something of her mother and father in the jasmine plant. She sensed a long distant history, a shadow of an explanation.

Sometimes, a bud that was just about to bloom would remind her of something. Her eyes would fill with tears.

And then, if her husband saw her misty eyes, he would ask with an understanding look, "It's the jasmine again, isn't it?"

Two Small Children

They sat together on the old pier gazing at the horizon. Their small feet didn't stop moving, swinging back and forth lightly and relaxed. Their high-pitched voices rang clearly, carried by the wind.

Occasionally, a ship's horn could be heard from the harbor. And a ship could be seen moving away from the pier. It wasn't busy anymore. No more bustling harbor noises. Just water lapping up against the concrete wall. Just the sound of old sampans tied to the harbor brushing against each other with each small wave. Sometimes bumping against each other.

They watched the ship sail further away. They gazed at the horizon. They stared into the distance while conversing.

"Naro," said the girl, "do you come here often?"

"Sometimes," the boy answered, "sometimes."

"This is the first time I've ever been here. My mother won't let me go anywhere after school."

"Your mother's good."

"I'm bored at home. Every day I have to study, study, study."

"Your mother's good, Isti."

"But I'm bored."

"My mother just plays cards."

A seagull flew overhead. Its screech was answered by other birds passing each other. The girl looked for something in her school bag. There was still a piece of bread spread with pineapple jam in her lunch bag.

"I'm hungry. Do you want half?"

The boy took the piece the girl offered. They ate the bread while watching each other.

"It's good," the boy said.

Isti just smiled. The ship was smaller now. In a little while it would disappear beyond the horizon.

"Have you ever gone sailing, Naro?"

"No. But my father does all the time. My father's a sailor."

"Do you want to be a sailor?"

"I want to sail. Go far away. But I don't want to be a sailor."

"You don't want to be like your father?"

"No!"

The girl appeared surprised to hear Naro's voice harden suddenly. But she still asked. Her eyes were bright. Their feet, dangling off the pier, brushed against each other occasionally.

"Where do you want to go, Naro? I always want to go far away too, but I don't know where."

"I don't know either. I just want to go."

"I want to know what's over the horizon."

"I do too."

The ocean waves splashed against the concrete under the old wooden pier. There was also the sound of wood creaking as the old sampans brushed against each other. The sun was still hot, but there was a strong breeze, so they did not feel too hot. They were tanned. The beach guard speedboat passed by and the guard yelled quickly.

"Ahoy! Don't play too close to the edge! It's dangerous!"

But he quickly passed. And the two children really didn't care. Naro, maybe eight years old, took off his school uniform and his shoes and jumped into the ocean.

"Isti! Come on in!" Isti, maybe seven years old, just shook her head and laughed. Naro teased her briefly with a splash, then he dove under the water surface.

The ocean bottom under the old pier was shallow and the water was clear. Isti could see Naro pick something up from the ocean floor and quickly push his way up to the surface.

"This is for you, Isti!"

Something rolled onto the pier. Isti ran to pick it up. It was just a flat rock, brownish because of the sunrays. Isti held it happily while running to the edge.

"Get another one, Naro! These stones are really beautiful!"

In a few minutes, there was a pile of rocks on the pier. Naro dressed and lay down using his school bag as a pillow. Isti chose the stones that she thought were beautiful. She put them in her bag. She threw the rest back into the ocean. One by one.

"Isn't your mother going to be looking for you, Isti?" Naro asked while lying down, still with his eyes closed.

"Just let her look."

"She'll be worried."

"Just let her be worried."

"You're not going home?"

"I'm not going home."

Naro opened his eyes. He searched at his friend's face, which was turned down towards the ground.

"I never want to go home. But, in the end, I always do," Naro said again.

Isti's head was still bent down. She was sitting on one of the pier posts.

"I don't want to go home," she sighed softly. Naro almost didn't hear her. The trucks rumbled through the streets in front of the giant warehouses. The clamor of ships docking. The sun was tilting to the west, its rays glistening on the surface of the ocean. Shimmering.

Naro got up. He straightened up his bag and clothes.

"I'm going home, Isti. You should go home, too."

Isti shook her head without lifting her face.

"Well then, I'm going home by myself. I'm hungry."

The girl didn't move. Naro took a step.

"I'm going home now. Are you going to school tomorrow?"

Isti lifted her face. She looked at Naro. She seemed to be storing something deep inside herself, but Naro did not realize it.

"I'm going home now. You should go home right now. Don't stay here too long."

Naro traced the wooden boards on the pier with the tip of his shoe. The wind dried his wet hair. They could hear people shouting in the harbor. The sounds of heavy objects falling. The sounds of cargo barge engines.

Isti did not want to look at Naro. Her glassy eyes were directed towards the ocean without seeing anything. She gazed towards the horizon, but she didn't see it. In her mind's eye she saw the mosquito net shaking back and forth. And she saw something inside the net, dimly in the darkness, but very familiar. Her eyes watered suddenly and Isti bent her head down again to hide her face. Her braids fell forward. She cried silently.

The ocean's whispers could still be heard lapping against the edge of the pier. And the sound of scratching wood, the old sampans brushing against each other, buoyed by the waves.

Suddenly Naro spoke, "Why are you crying, Isti?"

The girl pulled back. She saw Naro standing stiffly. She stopped crying. Her face was wet. There were still a few sobs trembling in her chest. She blew her nose in her handkerchief.

"Are you afraid to go home alone? I'll take you home."

Isti just shook her head.

"Are you mad at me?"

She shook her head again. Not knowing what else to ask, Naro stepped towards the edge of the pier. He squatted there, watching the little waves which came from who knows where. Isti wiped her tears away with her little fingers.

"Naro," the girl called out in a hoarse voice.

"Yeah?" Naro answered, still watching the water.

"Can you keep a secret?"

"What secret?"

"But you must promise not to tell anyone."

"Yeah, I won't tell anyone."

"Come here."

Naro drew near. Isti took hold of his two hands.

"You really won't tell anyone, will you, Naro?"

"Yeah, yeah. I promise, Isti."

The sun was approaching the horizon. A red glare reflected off the giant warehouse walls, shimmering like aged gold. The two children sat cross-legged on the pier facing each other. Isti told him what she saw the previous night.

"Are you sure the woman was your mother?" Naro asked. "Not another woman? A relative who was staying over maybe? Lots of my mother's friends spend the night. And sometimes they sleep in my mom's room and I make a mistake."

"No, there's no one else in our house. It must have been Mother. I know her voice. And I saw her vaguely. That man was kissing her. Madly. On her neck, on her mouth, on her chest. My mother seemed hurt, but just kept silent. Mother hugged him. Usually I never wake up at night, but I did last night. I dreamed that Father was alive again, buying me toy boats from Japan. When I woke up, I heard voices in my mother's room. I thought maybe Father really did come back to life. Ugh. That man was really scary. His body was full of pictures of skulls and words. I asked Mother this morning. Wow. She was really angry. I don't want to go home, Naro. I don't want to go home." Isti blurted out her story and repeated it several times.

Naro listened calmly to Isti's story.

"I don't want to go home, Naro. I don't want to."

Isti shook her head furiously. Her braids swung back and forth. But Naro's face remained unaffected. His eyes gazed into the distance.

"Just go home, Isti. That happens all the time."

"It does? Why did Mother slap me?"

"I see it almost every day, Isti. Daytime, evening, night. My mother sleeps with her card-playing friends. I also see her women card-playing friends sleep with her male card-playing friends. Switching around. If she's winning, my mother doesn't sleep, but if she loses, my mother sleeps with her friend. I got slapped the first time I saw her and asked. But I always see her and maybe she got bored scolding me. Mother just plays cards every day."

"Does your father know?"

"If my father comes home, my mother plays cards somewhere else."

"I just found out about it now, Naro. But my mother doesn't play cards. Mother tells me to study every day."

"I already said your mother is good, Isti."

The lanterns on the pier suddenly lit up. It seemed as if the two children wanted to catch something that had alluded them. They could see the blinking lights of ships in the harbor. The ocean looked like a puddle of red water. Naro saw Isti's braids like two black lines against the sun. The two were silent, feeling the breeze blowing and time crawling.

Suddenly, there was the screech of car brakes. They turned towards the street and the warehouse front. They could see a woman get out of the car and stride quickly towards them. She stopped at the edge of the pier; she didn't approach. A man sat behind the steering wheel in the car. He also looked in the direction of the two children.

"Istiiii!" The woman waved.

"Your mother?" Naro asked. Isti nodded.

"Istiii! Come on home! It's almost night."

Isti looked at Naro doubtfully.

"Just go home, Isti. You can tell me more tomorrow," said the boy, who suddenly felt grown-up.

"I...", said Isti, stopping. She wanted to say something, but couldn't.

"Tomorrow, Isti. Your poor mother..."

"Istiii! Come on!"

The girl seized her bag and ran. Naro watched the woman hug and carry Isti through the gloomy evening light. He watched the car drive off until it disappeared behind the row of giant warehouses. He suddenly felt very hungry.

The Tragedy of Asih, Wife of Sukab

Listening to the *dangdut* song: *Don't let it happen, my wandering life....* Drained of all her strength, Asih collapsed onto the dirt floor. It was damp and cold. The moist earth was covered with a sheet of newspaper. Asih's eyes were closed.

"Sukab, Sukab, where are you, Sukab," she whispered. She groped the area around her. She could feel clumps of dirt, pebbles, ant holes. She was splayed out in the dimness. Her breathing was labored. Then she fell asleep.

Evening passed and the space inside the hut became darker. A gloomy, empty room. Four, dark, square, woven bamboo slat walls. A pair of worn-out rubber slippers. A crumpled plastic bag with the word 'Nike' written on it, who knows what was inside. A sheet of newspaper.

A woman.

An exhausted, dull, pitiful woman. She wore a batik dress, the colors no longer vibrant, as if she had continuously worn only that dress for two years. Not brown, not white, and not gray either. Her hair was long, straight and reddish. The long, straight, reddish hair was tied back with a rubber band.

Asih slept soundly. Her soul was on a vacation from this tragic life. Listen to the heavy tired breathing! The soft snores crept through the emptiness. Darkened fate cast down in a darkened room. What was she dreaming about?

Her mouth was half open. It was attractive enough to kiss. But who would kiss passionately in a place that was as damp, dark, filthy, rancid, full of rat carcasses, and polluted as this place?

Soft, graceful moonbeams illuminating the filthy earth. Clogged sewers reflecting a silvery glow. Asih dreamed in her sleep.

"Sukab! Sukab! You've succeeded, haven't you, Sukab?" Asih shouted cheerfully.

Sukab emerged in the distance from behind the haze. Oh, Sukab, Sukab, Asih thought, I've never seen you as handsome as this. Where did you get your nice clothes, Sukab? Super clean. Super white. Radiant. I'm dazzled. You are wearing a tie, Sukab. Your hair shines, your eyes are bright, your face is clean, your smile is brilliant. I've never seen you look as self-assured and happy as this, Sukab. Am I dreaming, Sukab?

"Sukab! Sukab! I love you, Sukab! I care about you! I miss you! You've been gone so long! *So long!* People in our village miss you! They've all heard! You've become a success!"

Sukab smiled in the dream. He sat on a cloud that was part of a procession as if it were a golden train.

"Yes, this is me, Asih, my wife. It's me, your husband, Sukab! Not Sukab, the daily farmhand in Kepanjen, Tulungagung! But Sukab, the director of the mosquito coil factory! It's me, Asih, it's your husband, Sukab!"

"Oh, my God! So what they say is true, Sukab. You're a success!"

"Of course I've succeeded, Asih, I've become a 'real man'. Should I have become an insect? Ha ha ha ha!"

"I mean, I mean, you have lots of money, we have a beautiful house, a car, rice fields, stores, cattle, big plush sofa, a spacious bed where we can make love, a large teakwood cabinet that has a nightlight, a swimming pool, a helicopter, a match factory. But most important, Sukab, you are a respected person! You have status! I'm Javanese, aren't I, Sukab? Wealth, for me, is of secondary importance. Number one is respect! Respect, Sukab, respect!"

"Ha ha ha ha, you're getting smarter, Asih. Of course, I'm respected, Asih! What director isn't? What's more, the director of the most popular mosquito coil factory!

"You must know why my mosquito coils are so popular, Asih. People don't want their dreams to be interrupted. They want to dream without getting any mosquito bites. They need to dream! Life needs dreams, Asih! I've become rich because people want to dream. They want to dream about a good, respected life without mosquitoes. Be grateful to them, Asih. Fortunately, they consider dreams to be so important; they regard dreams as a necessity for life and those dreams may not be bothered by mosquitoes!"

"Oh, Sukab, Sukab! I love you, Sukab!"

"I do, too!"

"I love you!"

"I love you, too!"

"I miss you!"

"I miss you, too!"

"But you never come home, Sukab. Why? Why, Sukab? Why?"

The image of Sukab vanished. Asih woke up.

A remnant of happiness from the dream remained when she unintentionally looked up. The moon was visible beyond the glass roof tiles. But a strange feeling soon washed over her. Where am I? she wondered, lifting herself up from the newspaper that covered the damp earth. There was just enough light in the dim room from the moonlight that seeped through the glass roof tile to illuminate the lines of the bamboo thatch walls, and the plastic bag with unknown contents and the worn-out slippers.

Asih squatted. She moved her chin between her knees. She could hear voices. Where am I, she wondered again. She could hear voices of people talking. She could hear the sound of footsteps. She could hear faintly the sound of the television mixed with the radio. She could hear the sound of an orchestra. She could hear people laughing. She could hear it all, faintly.

She could also hear the sound of rats squeaking and chasing each other around the hut. She could hear the rustle of cockroaches on the thatched walls. She could hear the hum of those annoying mosquitoes buzzing in her ear. The length of her arm started to itch. Her leg started to itch. Her face also started to itch. Asih scratched her whole body. There were so many mosquitoes. There were so many cockroaches. There were so many rats. There were so many people who lived with mosquitoes, with cockroaches, with rats.

Asih was still scratching her itchy body. Then, she started to remember something.

"Asih! Asih!"

She had been planting rice in the middle of the paddy field. She saw Paidi wave from his bicycle in the middle of the street.

"Asih! I saw Sukab in Jakarta!"

She rushed over to Paidi. Her hands were still muddy.

"Did you really see him, Paidi? Where is he? Why doesn't he come home?"

"I saw him twice, but we didn't have a chance to talk."

"Why not?"

"Well, because the first time he was up on the truck and the second time I was the one on the truck."

"Up on what truck? Paidi, explain."

"Well, I was a day laborer, 'Sih. Every morning I had to be ready and waiting on the street. When an empty truck came by, we all scrambled to get on because the contractor needed only so many workers. So, that first time, I didn't get a place because there were already some people on the truck, including Sukab, your husband, Gothak's dad."

"Oh, Sukab, Sukab. What was he like, Paidi? Where did he sleep?"

"Yeah, just like me when I'm there, 'Sih. His clothes were smudged with dirt, carrying his own shovel or hoe every day. We worked in construction. You know, 'Sih, those tall buildings!"

"Sleep in the building?"

"No, that's not allowed. Maybe the contract laborers can, but the daily hire sleep in the streets, 'Sih, like the street people. You have to wake up really early and wait on the road. When an empty truck goes by slowly, jump on quickly. If not, well, you might not eat, 'Sih. Like the second time I saw Sukab, maybe he didn't get to eat that day. When he wanted to jump on, I was already on the truck from the previous stop where there were only three people. They needed five more. And Sukab was slow in jumping on, so I could only wave my hand at him. After that, we never met again."

Asih slapped a mosquito. Then she scratched her itchy body again. Oh Sukab, Sukab. Why don't you come home, Sukab? No news, no reports. Why are you embarrassed to be a daily laborer, Sukab? I wouldn't be embarrassed to be a construction worker. I'm Javanese. Respect is number one, wealth is number two, but if you don't get either, I can accept that, Sukab. What's more, you haven't given up. Paidi heard from your friends that you work like a crazy man. Almost every day, you work overtime in the skyscraper until midnight. I'm not embarrassed that you are a construction laborer. What's more respectable than hard work, Sukab? What? You can be loyal to life; why can't you be loyal to me? I won't force you to come home. You can go wherever you want; you can be whoever you want, but just let us know. I'm worried. Gothak asks, "Where's daddy? Where's daddy?" It's been two years since you were with us. Where are you, Sukab? Where are you?

She heard rats scurrying in and out of the sewers. Rats were creatures of God too. They were searching for food in the moonlight. Asih covered her face. Her thoughts wandered. Fortunately, the person who helped me at the Pulo Gadung bus terminal was so nice. I felt so lucky. Apparently, Jakarta was not so strange. When I got off the bus, I didn't know where to go or what to do. I thought Jakarta was like Tulungagung. Paidi had warned me not to go by myself if I didn't have an address. But I was determined. I had to find Sukab.

The man was friendly. He bought me a meal. He brought me here. He said he knew Sukab. He said he would look for Sukab. I was told to wait. To sleep first. He knew I was exhausted. He said that maybe Sukab would be at my side when I woke up. Ah, it was like a dream. Perhaps not as beautiful as my own dream, but still like a dream. There would be nothing better than seeing Sukab. There would be no better dream than embracing Sukab.

I'm awake now. No one is here. Maybe in a little while. That man is really nice. Fortunately, there still are good people in this world. In this life, we must help each other; if not, what would become of the world?

The door opened suddenly. Asih lifted her face. Black shapes filled the door. Her heart leapt.

"Sukab?"

There was no answer. Just the scratching of cockroaches on the thatch walls. The buzz of mosquitoes and the faint voices of people talking in the distance. The muddled voices of the radio mixed with the television mixed with an orchestra and the people gathered around the orchestra.

"*Mas?*" she called again. Still no answer.

Asih still did not suspect anything when as quick as a flash of lightening a firm hand covered her mouth, pulled her down to the ground, and something very heavy suddenly climbed on top of her. She tried to hit and kick, but four pairs of hands quickly pinned down her arms and legs. Then her cervix seared with pain. Incredible pain.

"Great!" said one voice, but Asih no longer could hear anything. She could only hiss.

"Sukab, Sukab, where are you, Sukab?"

At the construction site for an international hotel in the Jakarta jungle, a man was drenched with sweat from heaving boulders off a truck. He had decided that tomorrow he would go home to Kepanjen, Tulungagung, with the little savings he had collected, the result of his labor of two years. He decided that after the end-of-the-fasting month celebrations, he would move back to the city with his wife and child. Even though it was difficult and exhausting, he thought life was better in Jakarta.

From the sky, moonlight shone down on sweat-drenched Sukab. From the sky, moonlight shone through the glass roof tile on to sweat-drenched Asih, sprawled out and bleeding.

The Woman at the Bus Stop

S he stood there for ten years. Searching to her right with anxious eyes, waiting for a city bus that had just one seat for her. But a city bus with one empty seat never came.

A city bus would emerge from the right always leaning to the left because it was full, packed, with so many people hanging from the doorframes. Seeing this, the woman standing at the bus stop wouldn't get on the bus.

All of the people to her right and left also looked in the same direction. As soon as a bus emerged at the far end of the street, tension would fill their faces and even before the bus reached their stop, they would begin roughly and shamelessly jostling for a position. They did not speak to each other, but competed fiercely. One inch of space in the bus doorway was reason enough for a tussle.

At that stop, at every moment, people peered to the right, their faces full of hope. So did that woman.

I first met her ten years ago on a night train that left from the outlying district. The train was full and crowded and smelly and had lots of beggars on it, but there was a seat for that woman. Just by glancing at her, I could tell she felt tortured. With a long-suffering look, she repeatedly wiped away the sweat on her forehead and incessantly muttered a vague complaint. She had so many things—

suitcases, boxes tied up with raffia, plastic bags, bamboo-plaited cases, and who knows what else. Was she going to gamble her fate in Jakarta? The train and night bus spewed forth people leaving to try their fates in Jakarta every day.

We hadn't spoken all night, but when the train arrived at the final station, I helped her unload all of her things. I felt sorry for her. She was so pale, so thin. Her face was so weary and her skin so smooth. Surely she couldn't lift heavy things and wasn't accustomed to washing and perhaps not used to travelling by herself. Poor soul. I carried her things to the bus stop.

"Where are you going, *Mbak*?"

"Priok Harbor."

"You have so many things. Why don't you just take a taxi?"

"It's okay. I just want to take the bus. It's cheaper."

I wanted to say that it was difficult to ride the bus with so many things. I also wanted to lend her money if she really didn't have any. It wouldn't matter if she couldn't repay me, as long as she reached her destination safely. But her face signaled that she didn't want to be bothered. Perhaps she was afraid of being deceived. People are always suspicious of strangers. Perhaps I looked like one of the con men scattered all over Jakarta. What could I do? We shook hands and went our separate ways.

At the end of the street, I turned back to look at the stop. I saw the woman staring to the right with eyes full of hope, waiting for the city bus that would take her to her destination. All around her, people were looking in the same direction, waiting for the city bus to come, dragging because it was burdened with too many passengers.

One week later, I passed the same place.

"Hey, *Mbak*, why are you still here?"

"Yeah, because there aren't any empty seats."

"Ah, *Mbak*, it's really hard. That's how it is if you want to ride the bus. There often aren't any empty seats. That's usual, *Mbak*."

"But I don't want to stand. I'm tired. I'm not used to riding the city bus. I have to get a bus with one empty seat for me."

"What if I take you, *Mbak*? We can go in a taxi."

"No, no. Don't go to any trouble. I just want to take the city bus. It's cheaper."

"I'll pay for the taxi, *Mbak*. It's okay."

She didn't answer. Her eyes grew wider. Then she looked away. A city bus approached. Double-decker. From a distance it appeared to be leaning to the left. The woman was going to get on, but didn't. The upper level was full of passengers. The lower level was even more full. The staircase was packed with even more passengers. Both doorways were stuffed with people hanging from the doorframe. The conductor clearly yelled out the destination name.

"Get inside! Move over! Move over! There's still room! Come on, *Pak*! Move over, *Pak*! Yeah! You in the red shirt! Move over! Don't be selfish! Come on! Priok, still empty! Let's go!"

The conductor's voice was soon swallowed by the clamor of city noises. Muffler exhaust filled the air and the sun beat down without pity. Everyone looked miserable, grimacing in the searing heat. Their foreheads, necks and the backs of their clothes dripped with sweat. I wanted to say something to the woman, but she didn't give me a chance. I was stunned. She had been here for one week, waiting for a city bus with just one empty seat.

I looked at her things that were still piled up. It was pathetic. The people around her didn't care. People clutching folders. People in uniforms. People wearing veils. People who were dressed up. People who were wearing perfume and oil in their hair. Those people just stared expectantly towards the right, waiting for the city bus that would take them to their destinations. The city bus always arrived leaning to the left because it was too full and the two doorways clogged with passengers hanging from the doorframes. But people still tried to squeeze in, enter, elbowing, jostling, forcing, searching for an empty space—as tiny as it may be—for themselves.

Every time the city bus appeared lopsided and spewing black smoke at the far end of the street, the woman would stir as if she was going to try to grab a place for herself, but it never happened. She would look at the door packed with passengers hanging on, look at her things, look through the bus windows where some of the passengers were weak and sleepy because of lack of oxygen. She never moved whenever the bus stopped one or two seconds at the stop.

"That one, *Mbak*. The bus to Priok. Quick, get on."

"No. Later. There aren't any empty seats."

Oh my. *Mbakyu, mbakyuuuu.* How long are you going to wait? I started to think that the woman—who was actually fairly pretty and refined and sincere—was a bit crazy. It was useless to waste time on her. I left. I had to tend to my own matters.

"*Mbak*, just take a taxi. It'll be faster!" I yelled one more time, even though I knew it wouldn't have any effect. She looked at me briefly as if she was trying to consider it. She didn't answer, but I wasn't waiting for an answer. I hurried on. When I got to the end of the street, I glanced back one more time. She was still there.

It was evening. I walked on with that memory. The wide, blazing red sun sank behind the skyscrapers. The reddish-yellow rays shimmered towards the evening clouds. The woman stood there like a statue holding a plastic bag. The wind teased her dress and hair. How quiet it was there. How still. The people around her might have known her, but perhaps not. Their attention was focused to the right, waiting for the city bus that would take them to their destinations.

The days passed. Although she wasn't always in the forefront of my mind, I could never forget the woman who was still standing at the bus stop. Whenever I saw another woman carrying a plastic bag, I would remember her. It turned out that many women in Jakarta have dull faces, wear faded dresses and carry plastic bags. Actually, I never really paid attention to women like that, but ever since that woman at the bus stop entered my thoughts, I began noticing other women. I wanted to know if there were other women like that. And, apparently, there were indeed many women with dull, lifeless faces, wearing faded dresses, carrying plastic bags.

On an empty city bus in the quiet middle of the night, I let my mind wander. Who were the weary women with the lifeless faces and plastic bags? It seemed that I was watching actors in a gloomy play.

On the empty city bus, through a shower of light and ever-changing colors, I thought about the millions of people who slept soundly after a day of hard work. How a valuable life is snatched away. Three plates of rice every day, three cups of coffee, three bananas, and an array of thoughts. How expensive life is. If only we were never hungry. If only there was nothing called the stomach, food, life…

My empty city bus rumbled on, as if on a journey into the world of my dreams. Silent skyscrapers, fancy city lights flashed by, transforming the past. I saw myself hidden in the back seat. I saw myself as a stranger in the dirty windowpane. Who was that person who was swallowed in the commotion of the streets? Who was that? It was ten years of wandering from one city bus to another city bus. It was ten years of concentrating energy for just one empty seat.

My city bus went past the bus stop where the woman was still standing waiting for one empty seat. Unfortunately, my bus was going in the opposite direction. She still stood like a statue holding the plastic bags and her faded dress blowing in the wind. She was still there, but even she was quickly swallowed by the night and swept away into my past.

I remembered every woman I saw at every stop. Indeed, I was only a travelling salesman. I never stayed in any one place for very long. I often fell in love, but I was never loyal. I travelled in and out of villages, up and down mountains, up and down rivers, and along beaches. I sold items of daily necessities and big city dreams for my living. I didn't want to be rich. I just wanted to survive. I wanted to see many places. I wanted to hear many sounds. I wanted to smell a thousand and one of life's scents. How frightening it would be to be imprisoned in one place. How boring it would be. How disgusting. I always moved from place to place, even if only one step at a time. The places I've been to have been pleasant, but I realize that they are only memories. I know I've met people who are emotionally disturbed. It's always the same everywhere. People go crazy because of their own importance. I think everyone, at heart, is just a travelling salesperson, always doing everything for their own benefit. Life is a series of targets with different standard measurements. It's disgusting. I wanted to throw up. Huuueeek!

Was that woman also a travelling salesperson? Yes, yes, yes. Who was that woman? Where was she from? Where was she going? I asked and asked in my heart and tried to make sense of it. Was she someone in love, wandering after being left by her lover? Was she a wife who was frustrated and left her home because her husband was crazy? Was she a wife who had been divorced because she was barren and was trying her fate in the capital city? Was she a mother who had lost her child in a terrifying accident? Was she a woman who had just given birth to a child of an illicit relationship and was regretting throwing the baby away in a trashcan? Was she a woman who had lost her entire family in a single moment and now lived completely alone?

Perhaps she was the wife of a wealthy person and was just pretending to be crazy. Didn't rich people act strange sometimes? Isn't this life boring sometimes and we need surprises? Perhaps she was an unknown actress who was proving her ability to deceive everyone. Perhaps she was just a woman who was waiting for someone, who knows who, to appear, who knows when. Perhaps too, the woman really was a patient who had escaped from a psychiatric hospital. But she had the brains to survive in that place for ten years. Who knows what she would sell after her goods were traded away for food. Would she sell her body? She was white-skinned and had a fairly nice face and at every bus stop there were always people who would casually sleep with anyone with a fairly nice face, especially at night.

Who was she? Where was she from? Where was she going? Whose daughter was she? How many brothers and sisters did she have? Did anyone miss her and was anyone looking for her? Oh my God, what a life! What a journey!

I was still gliding forward on the empty city bus. My city bus was moving without a conductor and without a driver. I felt like I was riding a flying horse. I still remembered the woman who was, surely, still standing at the bus stop, staring to the right, waiting for the city bus with just one empty seat. She stood there for ten years. For ten years....

Semangkin (formerly Semakin)[1]

Sukab had forgotten when he started pronouncing the word *semakin* as *semangkin*. He felt that as a good Indonesian, he should not have any difficulty pronouncing *semakin*. Actually, that one word had never been a problem. The word *semakin*, like other words in Indonesian, was pronounced as *semakin*, not *semangkin*, without the nasalized 'n'. Sukab couldn't remember when the sound "ng" had snuck into his pronunciation. He tried repeatedly to pronounce *semakin*, but always heard himself say *semangkin*.

"Damn," he said to Santinet, his wife, "Why does it seem as if I have some government official's tongue?"

"Like some government official? What's wrong with that? Aren't government officials exemplary models for the society? What's more, aren't you an official now?"

Perhaps Santinet wanted to be seen as a wife who supported her husband's career. Sukab was indeed now an official. To be precise, a *lurah*. Not in a village, but in the city of Jakarta. Yes, a professional lurah. As soon as his neighbors knew he had been selected, even before he was officially installed, they began to call him *Pak* Lurah. Later, at his inauguration, Sukab would have to

---

[1] This story satirizes the tendency of public officials during the New Order to imitate former President Suharto's idiosyncratic pronunciation of Indonesian influenced by Javanese, in which single consonants were nasalized; hence the word *semakin* was pronounced *semangkin*. *Semakin* means "increasingly".

make a speech. That meant that he would be forced to pronounce the word *semakin*, which will be heard as *semangkin*. Oh, oh, how embarrassing!

"Since when?" Sukab was still asking.

"Maybe ever since you became the head of the neighborhood association. Ever since then you had to give speeches everywhere."

Since he became the head of the neighborhood association? Yes, perhaps that was it. It did feel as if he had started hearing the word *semangkin* after he was forced to give speeches here and there, for this and that, and for various occasions that he never really enjoyed.

"You're right. It was probably after I became the head of the R.T. neighborhood association. But why does it have to be *semangkin*? I want to say *sema... sema... sema... ng... kin*! Ah, it's so difficult! You know what I mean, don't you?"

Santinet tried to understand, but she couldn't think of a response. She felt that she would never know precisely why or whether her answer was true or not. She spoke anyway.

"You've been influenced by the officials' style. You want to give a good speech, but there aren't any good examples. The only examples are the ones you hear on the radio or television, or the way the former lurah spoke. And in those speeches, there is, indeed, no word *semakin*. What there is, is the word *semangkin*. Have you ever heard the speeches of former President Sukarno?

"Not even once!"

"There! You see!"

Sukab nodded while sipping his coffee.

He thought that Santinet was a good lurah's wife. The previous day, Santinet had told him that, in the matter of language, the truth lay in what was alive in the community, not in the Indonesian language lessons on the television. Damn, thought Sukab, that was truly unheard of. What would his wife learn in the monthly Women's Association meetings?

Santinet came to keep him company. She brought warm fried bananas, still steaming.

"Please have some, Pak Lurah," she smiled coyly.

Sukab was delighted with her good mood. He seized a fried banana and swallowed it without chewing.

Suddenly, from outside the window, they heard their children shouting together, "Pak Lurah…!"

The day of Sukab's inauguration was approaching. Sukab was determined to pronounce the word *semakin* as *semakin*, not *semangkin*. He wanted to set the example. Actions were indeed important, but words were important too. The wrong words could be misleading. If everything that was wrong was considered right, what would happen to the country? Sukab was serious about this.

Every morning, while jogging, Sukab tried diligently to pronounce the word *semakin* properly. The housemaids who were already awake could hear Sukab practicing in the still empty streets:

"*Se–se! Ma–ma! Kin–kin! Semangkin!* Oh no, that's wrong! *Se–se! Ma–ma! Kin–kin! Se-mang-kin!* Damn it! Wrong again! *Se-se! Ma-ma! Kin-kin! Semangngngng….* ah! *Se-se…*"

It seemed that the persistence of the Revered *Semangkin* could not be overcome. Besides practicing while jogging, Sukab also tried pronouncing it in calmer situations. He would isolate himself in a quiet place and practice very slowly.

"*Sssseeeeeeemmmmmaaaaaaaa…*"

He could already feel the syllable "kin" on the tip of his tongue, but when he pronounced it, the "ng" still snuck in somehow.

" *… aaa… ngngngngng-kin* !"

Sukab did not give up. He went to his former classmate, a psychologist who usually wrote about a variety of problems in magazine forums.

"Tell me, Ji, why can't I pronounce the word *seeemaaaaa-ngngng…* ah! See, it's impossible just to explain it."

"I understand. You are not the first person who has come to me about this."

"What do you mean?"

"Yes, it's like this. Whenever someone is promoted to a position that requires them to speak officially in the public, with or without a text, the word *semakin* always slides into *semangkin*."

"How many people before me?"

"Oh! Just count how many government officials there are in this country. They all caught the condition I call 'The *Semangkin* Syndrome'."

"The *Semangkin* Syndrome?"

"Exactly! That's the title of my dissertation that is going to be evaluated next month, 'The *Semangkin* Syndrome: The Psychological Effect of Government Officials who Must Speak in Public and the Influence on the Development of the Indonesian Language.'"

Sukab was stunned. So he was just one victim. Ji, his friend the psychologist, had studied no less than 2,500 test cases in his research, and this was just a small percentage of the total number of cases.

"Have any of your patients recovered, Ji?"

Ji, the social psychologist with frizzy hair, peered seriously at Sukab.

"Usually, I give them two alternatives. First, just to accept the word *semangkin* and pronounce it with full determination. Or, to refuse it with courage by hating those who pronounce *semangkin,* who have adopted the attitude of a dog barking at the hard work of the linguists who have produced the official rules of the Indonesian language."

"What do the majority choose?"

"They all choose the first alternative. It appears that they all deeply love the officials who pronounce the word *semangkin*. Ha ha ha ha!"

Depressed, Sukab returned home. His wife, Santinet, was waiting again with a cup of hot coffee and warm fried bananas. Despite this, Sukab did not greet her enthusiastically. Apparently, this case of *semangkin* was not a light matter. It involved national discipline, decided Sukab. It involved national mentality and social concerns.

"Perhaps we could speak in public without pronouncing the word *semaaaaangng...* oh! Perhaps we could avoid that word?"

Santinet tried to recall the speeches of officials on the radio and television and even those delivered during surprise visits to the villages.

"Maybe it is possible to avoid it, Sukab, but if we want to speak like public officials in general, that word would be difficult to avoid. If an official speaks in public, that means he must mention 'development'. And development infers development that is 'increasing' in every way. It could be *semakin* awe-inspiring, *semakin* great, or *semakin* wonderful. In essence, it is development which is *semakin*, or in your pronunciation, development which is *semangkin*. Is there ever development that is not *semangkin*?"

Sukab dipped his fried banana in his coffee, then blew on it because it was still hot. Santinet was always right, he thought. Twenty years of marriage had taught him that women did indeed think more clearly than men. Perhaps we should trust women more in the future, he thought again and again. Despite that, Sukab's decision was firm: he should pronounce the word *semakin* as *semakin*, not *semangkin*.

"I don't want to just follow along, blindly imitate, or play it safe. I must hold on to the conviction that the word *semangkin* is really not suitable to be pronounced by a public official. I must pronounce it *semaaa ... ngng-kin!* Oh, no!"

Sukab practiced every day. He strove to pronounce the word *semakin* clearly and properly even in his heart. His neighbors who saw him screaming while he was jogging began to wonder if Sukab was emotionally disturbed. One of the neighbors caught Sukab by surprise while he was talking to himself in a quiet spot, providing the neighbor with more convincing evidence.

"He's been stressed ever since he was chosen to become lurah."

"Hey, don't be ridiculous. It's not stress."

"What is it then? Why is he going crazy?"

"Shh! This is Ji's doctoral research project. He's studying the *Semangkin* Syndrome."

It turned out that Sukab's battle was a difficult one. As an official, even at the sub-district level, it was not easy to reject matters that were considered customary, general, usual, and permissible in administering the government, like pronouncing *semakin* as *semangkin*.

One of his friends reminded him, "Hey, Sukab! I heard that you want to pronounce *semangkin* as *semakin*."

"Yes, I want to speak Indonesian correctly. If our speech is incorrect, then how can we account for our actions?"

"Be careful, Sukab. It could be could be seen as an insult to your superiors."

"Insult? What are you talking about? How can doing what is right be insulting?"

"Oh, don't be naïve, Sukab. Nowadays truth can appear to be a farce. If you're different all by yourself, it could be interpreted that you aren't in sync with everyone else, that you're making fun of everyone, or that you're truly, truly stupid."

"Oh, no, I'm confused by what you're saying. So, you're saying that pronouncing a word correctly is wrong?"

"Actually, it's still right. It is the truth, but it would be considered wrong. These days everything must be uniform, harmonious, and not threaten stability. Essentially, don't do anything unusual."

"Is speaking the truth unusual?"

"Yes, it's unusual! If you really want to know! It's unusual!"

After his friend left, Sukab struggled to understand the conversation.

Suddenly, a joyous shout was heard from Sukab's house.

"I did it! Ha ha ha! I did it! Ha ha ha! *Se-ma-kin!* *Se-ma-kin!* *Se-ma-kin!* Ha ha ha! *Semakin!*"

Early that morning, his wife, Santinet, gave him a warm kiss on the cheek.

"Thank goodness you've succeeded. I've always prayed for your success in pronouncing the word *semakin*.

Doctoral candidate Ji conveyed his congratulations over the telephone.

"I heard you've succeeded. Congratulations! Your case proves my hypothetical therapy, doesn't it?"

Sukab did not forget to give his thanks to God because he was able to speak the truth.

"Let's have a *selamatan*. We'll sacrifice a buffalo!"

Now Sukab felt ready to be installed as lurah. He would be able to work confident that he could do everything correctly. He felt it was time to show the public that not all civil servants were sloppy. There were also government officials who worked with energy and dedication, even on matters that seemed minor, like pronouncing the word *semakin*. Everything started with the little things, Sukab thought. The big changes would evolve later, on their own.

He had already typed his speech. He didn't want it to be written by anyone else. There were many *semakin*'s in his speech text because he was sure that he could pronounce it correctly. Yes, where was there development that wasn't *semakin*?

He was re-reading his text in his office when one of the clerks presented him with a letter stamped IMMEDIATE. He quickly opened the envelope and read the letter.

"Impossible!" Sukab screamed.

How could such a letter be sent?

It is hereby announced that the word SEMAKIN has officially been replaced with the word SEMANGKIN. Officials are required to use the word SEMANGKIN at formal functions and the word SEMAKIN is forbidden. This regulation takes effect as of today. It is hoped that it will be executed in good faith.

The announcement was signed by the Junior Minister of Acronyms and Basic Terminology.

"Impossible!" Sukab screamed again. He realized that Santinet was right again, that it was better to standardize the terms that lived in the community rather than push forward new terms. Damn it! Can I retrain my tongue? He wondered.

Slowly, Sukab tried to pronounce *semangkin*.

"*Seeeeemmmaaaa ... kin!*"

He failed!

For the entire day, Sukab tried doggedly to say *semangkin*, but he consistently failed. The sound "ng" would not come out of his mouth. Every time he said *semangkin*, it came out *semakin*.

Damn it! Damn it! Sukab thought over and over again. Sweat drenched his entire body. He had to give his speech tomorrow. Damn! All day, he telephoned here and there. None of his friends and acquaintances, including the doctoral candidate, Ji, could help. Day passed into night. Damn! What would happen with his competency report if he didn't read every word *semakin* in his text as *semangkin*? Newly installed and already making mistakes!

"Santinet, my wife, help me! I can't pronounce the word *se-ma-kin!* Oh, no, wrong again," he moaned.

Santinet, with her wise smile, stroked Sukab's head.

"Oh, Sukab, Sukab, my dear husband. You poor man; trying to hold up the truth. But the truth did not choose to side with you. You must learn to read the signs of the times, Sukab, my husband. That is the best and only way to live safely. Don't be too idealistic; don't be stubborn. Work well; try not to rock the boat. We don't live in an age of hard-headed heroes, Sukab, my husband. What we need now are merchants! Businessmen! Business!"

"Santinet, my wife, why are you lecturing me? I just want to be able to pronounce the word *semaaana... kin!* Ah!"

Santinet the wise, Santinet who always smiled and was capable of handling all problems, patted Sukab's shoulder.

"Be calm, Sukab, my husband. Hand everything over to me. Trust me. Everything will be alright."

So, on inauguration day, the one to step up to the podium was... Mrs. Sukab! Santinet represented her husband brilliantly by reading the text of his speech. Her voice was soft and persuasive, impressing the audience, as if they were listening to a lullaby singing reality to sleep. And, apparently, Santinet did not just read her husband's text, but she also slipped in her own opinions here and there, and even amended the text into an inspiring speech. The conditions of development were inflamed by her words. The listeners were seized by an rousing spirit to work.

Pak Camat whispered to his trusted employees.

"Perhaps she can replace her husband in the next term. Arrange her nomination."

"Yes sir!"

Santinet, the honorable Mrs. Sukab, was still speaking from the podium. All the words *semakin* were pronounced *semangkin.* There were no mistakes.

III
Whose Baby is Crying in the Bushes?

The Sun

The sky was still dark. However, as usual, the market was already beginning to wake up. The glow of lanterns, torches, and pressure lamps mixed with the neon lights on the electricity poles and the Chinese stores that were still closed illuminated the market activities in the street intersection. The ground was muddy and the lights were reflected in puddles of the night's rain. Suddenly, a young man on a motorcycle zipped out of the night and muddied puddle water splashed the face of a vegetable vendor who immediately swore at the driver. She cursed the ancestors and even descendants of the motorcycle rider to be tortured to his doom in hell. The noises and voices of the market started to buzz. The rumble of the engines of trucks that were unloading baskets of vegetables stirred a vagrant who had been sleeping in front of a store. After relieving himself in a corner while yawning and scratching his head and peering around vacantly at the world, he curled up again in the storefront.

The sky was still dark. Three goats were dragged in. A rooster crowed. The women vendors shouted back and forth. The bell-ringing of *becak* carts bearing heaps of vegetables with the vendors sitting atop the bundles interjected with the *jaipongan* music on the radio that was played in the noodle stall. People loitered around the food stall and ordered instant noodles, coffee, half-cooked eggs, or milk with raw eggs and honey. The vendors set their produce out on the ground or along the sidewalks, exposing their hopes and laying themselves vulnerable to their fates, which were so uncertain in those days. Some people greeted each other, some people wiped their dull eyes and sat down drowsily next to their produce, and some others began to quarrel. The eyes of one potato vendor were attracted to the firewood seller's swinging hips. The police patrol car passed by slowly with its red light flashing.

The sky was still dark. The air was still chilly. In another storefront, two market watchmen were still playing cards with the neighborhood security guard. People loitered, squatting near the cigarette seller. And the cigarette seller, without being asked, offered them clove cigarettes. Without waiting too long, they took them and slipped them behind their ears. A woman of the night who kept a room at the far end of the market descended from a passing taxi. Sacks thudded as they were thrown off oxcarts. The scents of all kinds of vegetables and spices began to invade the senses. An elderly woman vendor swearing and throwing a large shallot at a cat that stole a cut of salted fish. A dog with scabies barked for no reason. The sunrise prayer from the mosque could be heard. A locomotive engine thundered by without any cars attached.

The sky was still dark. The news broadcast began to flow forth from a transistor radio in the food stall. A car bomb exploded in West Germany killing an industrialist. Three Palestinian guerillas died, shot by an Israeli navy patrol. The first spine bone marrow bank in New York was established. President Hafez Assad of Syria telephoned Libya's leader, Muammar Gaddafi, regarding the visit of Israeli prime minister, Shimon Perez, to Morocco. British prime minister, Margaret Thatcher has softened her stance of opposition to economic sanctions on South Africa. The Playboy empire was going bankrupt. Argentinean soccer player, Diego Maradona, was vacationing in Tahiti. American President Ronald Reagan warned of the communist danger in Central America. The film, *Ibunda*, won nine Citra awards, the Indonesian aspirant of the Academy Awards. The total number of victims of the Chernobyl nuclear reactor leak was growing. Actress Liz Taylor declared that she was still open to falling in love. Then, the news broadcast was closed with an announcement: *Attention. As of today, the sun will not rise again. Please take note.*

The sky was indeed still dark. Several people in the food stall who had been paying attention to the broadcast were stupefied. They looked at each other in bewilderment. The food they had swallowed stuck in their throats. It didn't make any sense. The days always passed by without any meaningful changes. This was only the news. If you hadn't heard it, it wouldn't have mattered. So, why care about an announcement that was read so nonchalantly? The people in and around the food stall surely heard it, but were not prepared for an announcement like that. In fact, the sound of the radio for them was just one of the myriad of noises of the market that they had heard for years without one single change! Those people who had by chance been paying attention to the radio and were startled by the news quickly resumed eating even though a puzzled look remained on their faces. The sun will not rise again? Was that possible? It didn't make any sense. This was surely a misplaced portion of a radio drama. Or an ad for batteries.

But the sky was indeed still dark. Life went on as usual. Shortly, the sky would become lighter. And the shoppers would come. And the sun would rise higher. And the dust would fly. And the trash would scatter. As it always did. Disgusting. The sweaty coolies lifting sacks and crates. The security guards and watchmen blowing their whistles. One gulp of an ice drink at mid-morning. Later. It would happen. Surely. In this life, the sun was a certainty. Everything else was pure fate. The vendors were ready for the buyers. They looked up at the sky. It was still dark.

Suddenly, someone jumped onto a truck bed. He raised his arms up and spread out his fingers. And he shouted.

"Listen, my brothers and sisters! Repent! The end of time has come! The sun is no more! Repent while you can!"

He was a handsome young man. His hair was wavy and long. His clothes were tattered. His face glowed. The people near him stopped working. The people in the food stall who had heard the broadcast were startled. Their faces were still full of questions.

"Listen, my brothers and sisters! I appeal to you, beg for forgiveness from God right now! The sun is not going to rise! This is the last day of human civilization! Repent! Ask for forgiveness for your lives, which have been smeared with sin, so that you will escape the tortures of Hell! Escape the torture of a terrifying Judgment Day! Repent! Before God's punishment makes you suffer! My brothers and sisters! Repent! My brothers and sisters…"

Some people stopped what they were doing. They drew nearer and watched the speaker carefully. The coolies on the truck were confused. They didn't know what to do with the fellow who was shouting. Several of those who gathered around the truck began to recognize the speaker.

"Hey, it's Sukab!"

"Yeah! It's Sukab!"

"How crazy!"

"Damn him! I thought it was for real!"

The crowd dispersed quickly. The two market guards who had been playing cards jumped up onto the truck. They slapped Sukab in the face and dragged him over to the guard station. Several people who didn't understand what was happening asked, "Sukab? Who's Sukab?"

"You know, Sukab, the crazy guy who laughs by himself at the electrical relay station."

"Oh, the crazy guy who likes to sing *Walang Kèkèk*?"

"Yeah!"

"Oh, he's nuts! But he was talking like a normal person, wasn't he? Like someone giving a sermon."

"Ah, no, no way! He was just like a crazy person!"

"Yeah! A crazy person! How could he say the sun wasn't going to rise today?!"

As they were speaking, they looked up. The sky was indeed still dark. For an instant, their hearts stopped. But they quickly forgot about it. In a little while, the sky would lighten. Just as it usually did. Just like dozens of years, hundreds of years, even millions of past centuries. Why should they get upset over a crazy man's speech? Some people even began to count the profits they would make that day. Their fingers danced nimbly on their calculators. The food stall was packed. The transistor radio pounded out a *dangdut* melody.

oh the cruelty of this world
not as cruel as your heart, oh – a – oh —

They forgot about the incident. The conversation at the food stall warmed over the rumors about the chicken farmer's widow. There was word that she was starting to eye the *tempe* vendor. Then they also talked about the problem of the supermarket that was going to be built. Eviction. Fire. Floods. Credit. Rice fields. Chicken. Progress. Japanese cars. Village women. Elections.

The sky was still dark. Several people began to feel that something unusual was happening. Usually, even though it wasn't light yet, at least there would be a glow on the eastern horizon. The sky would be turning purple with streaks of red, then gradually the world would become brighter. People would come out of their houses. The streets would fill up. And the market would become very lively.

But the sky was still dark. The people who were squatting at the food stall began to feel as if they had wasted too much time.

They looked at the clock and were startled. The sky should be light already. They looked at each other without speaking. They were afraid that if they uttered anything, it would become reality. They swallowed. Their faces paled when the dangdut song ended and the radio broadcaster read an announcement. The market suddenly became silent.

They gathered. The volume of the radio was increased so that others could hear and join in the concern that seemed would be too heavy if undertaken alone. The sound of the woman broadcaster's voice, gentle, soft, smooth, and subdued, announced: *Today, the sun will not rise. It will appear tomorrow—from the west.*

How calmly she read the announcement. As if she was making a weather prediction. Her tone was so normal. So routine. Was the broadcaster playing a trick? But this was the second announcement. So Sukab was right. No wonder his face was radiant. Perhaps he had received a revelation. Who knows. Damn! Rise in the west? What did that mean? Doomsday? The market was suddenly buzzing with panic. Anxious faces looking up at the sky. Indeed. The sky was pitch-black. The clouds rolled by like giant animals. The wind raged, cold and wild. The sound of branches snapping.

"God!" someone suddenly screamed. He knelt down and bent forward, both arms extended forward, head to the ground. "Forgive me, Lord!"

But someone scolded at him.

"It's just a little thing. Don't overreact! This is just nonsense. How can it be that the sun will not rise? Do you believe that crazy Sukab? Do you believe that radio drama? Bunk! Get back to work! Serve the customers! The sun will rise! For sure!"

"Yes! It will! But from the west! Know-it-all! Can you keep the sun from rising in the west? Do you know what it would mean if the sun rises in the west?" He snarled.

"Oh, so you believe that ridiculous nonsense? Have you gone crazy? Like Sukab?"

"Hey, look! Where's the sun?"

"Yeah, where's the sun?"

"Give me back the sun!"

He was quiet for a moment. But he still insisted.

"I don't know why the sky is still dark. I can't explain it. I'm just a vegetable merchant. I still don't believe the sun won't rise. What's more, rise in the west."

"Then what will happen?" a security guard asked.

"There's a troublemaker."

"Subversive?"

"Maybe. Why not?"

Suddenly, the security guard instructed: "Arrest any suspicious person!"

Not one person moved. People started to step, rather, in the direction of the guard, who retreated fearfully.

"Bastard! Traitor! You'll die!"

In the blink of an eye, the guard was attacked.

But that did not solve the problem. The sky was still dark. People looked up with worried faces.

"Sun! Sun! Oh, where have you gone?" screamed a desperate woman.

"Oh, God! What must we do?"

"What can we do?"

"We are only little people!"

"Should we ask for forgiveness now?"

"Is it true the sun will rise in the west, God?"

"Is today Doomsday, Lord?"

Someone leapt onto the truck. He screamed loudly over all the others.

"Brothers and sisters! This is the last day for us to repent! Tomorrow the sun will rise in the west. Judgement Day has come!

The sky will fall! Mountains will erupt! Rivers will overflow! Typhoons! We will all die! This is our last chance! Last chance to repent and lessen our sins! Every day we only think about seeking our own profits! Never attending to the fates of other people! Come, let's ask for forgiveness together while we still have a chance!"

People stared at him in confusion. Some, even though they were horrified to see the dark sky, were not convinced that the next day would be their last.

Someone else leapt onto the truck.

"Don't believe him! Don't believe what he says! Don't pay any attention to him! Come on and work! Don't waste any time!"

But the people didn't move.

Then, a third person jumped on to the truck.

"Be calm! Be calm! Now, this is what we'll do. Let's think more calmly. Don't panic! God loves those who are patient. Now, this is what I mean. None of this is for certain, right? It's not for certain that the sun will rise in the west. But, it's also not certain that it will rise in the east, right? So, let's just wait. If there's light in the west tomorrow, we'll rush to beg for forgiveness. If the sun rises in the east, we'll just work again as usual. How about that? Agreed? It's practical, isn't it? As merchants we have to think of our profits and losses, don't we?"

People's faces brightened. They had found a solution. They answered in unison.

"Agreed! It would be a waste if we asked for forgiveness now!"

"That's right. We'll just do it later if it's certain that we're going to die!"

The third person on the truck shouted again.

"Brothers and sisters, how about if we look for confirmation in the west?"

Then, as if moved by a mysterious force, the people with questioning faces started to move towards the west. They walked westward with worried looks on their faces. The market was soon deserted. The only person left was the vagrant man sleeping cuddled up in the storefront. Everyone walked westward. Sellers of potatoes, carrots, cabbage, firewood, instant noodles, as well as the owners of the sundry store, all hurriedly strode towards the west.

The sky was still dark. They headed to the west without stopping. A cold wind blew fiercely, sweeping dry leaves into the air. Along the street, people who were just waking up looked out from behind their doors and windows.

"What is it?" asked someone.

"We want to see the sun rise in the west," answered someone else. And the people who were just awakening looked upward. The sky was indeed still dark.

From house to house all along the street, people joined the group from the market, walking hurriedly en masse towards the west. Their faces were anxious and full of questions. In time, the line grew longer. Each person they met joined the group. Everyone headed to the west. They stepped steadily over the muddy ground, past pockets of puddles filled with the night's rainfall. They left the dry, barren skyscraper jungle and headed out of the city.

Outside the city, people from various directions thronged towards the west. Hundreds, thousands, even millions of people from all directions moved westward. Humans, animals, and vehicles jostled one another moving in the same direction. Trucks, buses, oxcarts, elephants, and camels joined with the sea of people flowing towards the direction where the sun usually set. Everyone experienced the same problem. Where, oh where was the west? Even those in the west moved west.... In the air, millions of birds and bats fluttered westward. Hundreds of millions of fish in the ocean and rivers swam towards the west. All the creatures on the face of the earth, in the water and in the air, moved in one direction. Humans no longer thought about their daily jobs.

Everyone, shadowed by fear, anxiety, and unanswered questions, thought about the sun.

The sky was still dark. The procession ended at a bay. When the group from the market arrived at the beach, there were already countless millions of people waiting there. They sat along the sand dunes gazing towards the west. Whispering waves lapped the shore. The beach was situated between two cliffs that were also covered with people. Birds crowded in all of the coconut trees and mangrove clusters. Bats hung in the trees and caves. Hundreds of millions of fish and water creatures swam in the ocean and river mouth. Clouds rolled along as if intending to destroy life. Everyone, every creature gazed westward. Waiting. Waiting.

Suddenly, who knows from where, Sukab appeared. He stood at the edge of the shore facing the people. His face was handsome and radiant. His hair was long and wavy. His clothes were tattered. Again, he started to lecture.

"My brothers and sisters! Repent! The sun…"

Those who knew him were startled.

"Hey, it's Sukab!"

"Yeah, Sukab!"

"Sukab? Who's Sukab?"

"You know, the crazy guy who likes to laugh by himself at the electric relay station."

"Oh, the crazy one who likes to sing *Walang Kèkèk*?"

Many people were ready to curse him, but as if he had reminded them about something, almost in unison, they turned to look skyward. The sky was still pitch-black.

A journalist covering the event interrupted:

"It can be asked, what is the difference between healthy and crazy?"

And all those people stayed there. Waiting. Waiting.

Marble Man

He was the eternal child. He was one hundred years old, but he never appeared to age. He was always small, like a young child, and looked like a child of eight years. No one knew exactly when or where he was born, or who his mother and father were. All of a sudden, one hundred years ago, there he was wandering everywhere. My grandfather and grandmother knew him too. His playmates grew older with time, but he always stayed the same. Short and appearing to be about eight years old. He wandered from neighborhood to neighborhood, challenging everyone to play marbles.

"Look, he's coming again!"

"Hey, Marble Man!"

"Amazing, he never gets old, yeah?"

"Yeah! Amazing!"

"He's not human! He's an angel!"

"Are angels really like that?"

"Just look, he's eternal."

"He's not an angel! Angels aren't like that!"

"Like what?"

"He's Marble Man!"

He walked from neighborhood to neighborhood dragging a huge sack filled with marbles. These were all of the marbles he had won over one hundred years. He had defeated marble champions from all corners of the world. Children became adults and new marble champions emerged, but not one was able to defeat Marble Man.

Adults challenged him. It was in vain. The diamond marble in his hand seemed to have eyes. Not one target had ever escaped his aim. Everyone just raised their hands and surrendered. And whenever he won, he would leave with an additional marble in his sack. Even though the sack was heavy because it was filled with all the marbles he had collected over one hundred years, he dragged it along with determination. The sack never tore even though it had been pulled all over the world for one hundred years.

Marble Man was like a memory. The past constantly returning again and again. He always appeared initially as a shadow. Pleasant, impressive, enchanting, then gone. He disappeared at the end of every alley in every neighborhood. Wherever there was a marble game, Marble Man would appear. Childhood dreams would be enacted. At the horizon, he would wave his hand, leaving behind all of the children he had defeated. No one would ever equal him. He was the true marble champion, the eternal child, sent from the heavens as a sign.

"Damn! He always wins!"

"I've trained for ten years. I've strung out my childhood just to defeat him, but he always wins."

"Fate sides with him."

"Yes. Fate sides with him."

"Doesn't he get tired of playing marbles? What does he get for being the eternal marble champion? Why does fate side with him?"

"I'm amazed too. Why does he do it?"

"But everyone lives to win!"

"That's why everyone dreams about beating him even though they know it's impossible."

"That's why there are marbles."

He did indeed come from the sky, but who knew which sky. Several people tried to follow him, but he always disappeared without a trace, even his footsteps. He vanished in between drifters' huts under bridges. He disappeared in corridors of high-rise buildings. He was whisked away, swallowed by the city bus that sped off to the capital city jungle. Every attempt to pursue him failed with the blink of an eye.

Some people preferred to forget about him because just thinking of Marble Man caused headaches. But the memories would not stay away because he always reappeared whenever people started to forget about him. His face was always fresh and pure. His eyes were clear and bright. His skin clean. His cheeks chubby. His hair black with bangs on his forehead. He always smiled and his voice was cheerful. He was light-hearted; a pleasing child.

He always appeared during the marble season. Joining the children as they positioned their marble pairs and threw their own eye marble, and then suddenly he was playing. His diamond marble was exquisite, sparkling under the lights or in the sun.

"There is no day without marbles," he said once. People just smiled. They accepted his appearance as a miracle that could occur in such difficult and troubled times as the one they were in. It was something different. It was entertainment. It was a surprise. Life wasn't only waiting for death, which was predestined to win.

He was already one hundred years old. My grandparents knew him too. But was it true that he would live forever?

"Aren't you tired of living?" I asked him one day. I was the one and only child in the whole world who never played marbles. That meant that I was the one and only child in the whole world whom he had never defeated. He always appeared whenever I thought about him. And he always appeared as a fond memory, suddenly slipping into my brain uninvited.

Marble Man didn't answer. He let me wonder and then disappeared before I could respond. It had been a long time since I was a child, but he would often appear to me no matter where I was.

"*Pak, Pak!* There's a visitor, *Pak!*"

"Who?"

"A small child, *pak*, dragging a sack!"

Sometimes he would appear in the elevator when I was alone. He'd appear in the glass window of my office on the seventeenth floor. He'd emerge from under the ground in my quiet, secluded rented room. He'd be sitting in the chair at my side, whether in a movie theater or on a flight to Venezuela. It was bizarre. It seemed as if he knew that I would never be bored, even though I didn't like marbles.

Once I was eating pizza when all of a sudden he was at my side. Marble Man smiled.

"Hey, where did you come from?"

He reached for a slice of pizza off my plate. Then he spoke of distant countries that were as beautiful and strange as those in fairy tales. Every time I heard him speak it was as if I were listening to a song. Indeed, he was not of the real world. I could never really believe him. I could only experience him as a part of something beautiful and touching.

Watching his steps, slow and growing distant, dragging his sack, I always felt that a part of me was being hauled away.

I often mused from behind the window of my seventeenth floor office while looking down at life on the ground. Watching lines of cars at gas stations holding up traffic. Watching people stream by on the sidewalks wanting to get home and wary of getting caught in the rain. Watching the weakening strands of the sunrays struggling with the glow of electric lights. How long will Marble Man endure?

I often saw him in neighborhood alleys, dragging his sack, looking for opponents. Sometimes I saw him when he was squatting at the edge of a circle with his diamond marble, cutting down all of his opponents mercilessly. There had never been anyone able to defeat him. He was invincible with no worthy opponent.

"Marble Man! Lose a game! Just once!"

"Yeah, just once, lose a game."

"Why win all the time?"

"Yeah, what for?"

"You're greedy! You don't want to lose and you don't want to grow old! You don't even know who you are! Remember, you're one hundred years old!"

"You should have done something to serve your country!"

"But you only play marbles!"

"Crazy marbles!"

"Crazy Marble Man!"

Apparently, it was difficult to whole-heartedly accept another person's superior achievements. People started to question one-sided fate.

"I ask you, Lord, why do you let Marble Man win all the time?"

"Why is he better than us?"

"We are Your servants too, Lord. Let us win just once."

"Yes, just once. It doesn't have to be often."

But the thunder just continued. Rain clouds rumbled by and a downpour drenched the people praying in the field. They scattered, looking for shelter. The field became deserted. The only one left there was Marble Man, enjoying the rain, laughing and playing.

I was stunned. These people were truly obsessed with marbles, as if they had nothing else to do. If they were still children, it would be understandable, but many of them were adults. Perhaps marbles were not the real issue here. These people needed something other than food-procuring activities. They needed something more entertaining. Life was too routine and boring. There had to be something that would take them away from the realities of daily life.

I saw all kinds of offers for dreams in the streets. Flyers for the lottery fluttering in the breeze, offering hope-filled dreams. People crowding into entertainment halls. Billiards, bowling, and video games everywhere. In air-conditioned rooms that were stuffy with cigarette smoke, people were intently focused on a glass screen placed directly in front of them. They screamed uncontrollably. They fought hard to win at games so that they could experience instant success.

People started to forget marbles. What's more, they forgot about Marble Man, who had always smashed their dreams of becoming champions.

I was thinking about all of this when suddenly he emerged on the other side of the windowpane. He had climbed up to the seventeenth floor like Spiderman. Like a giant lizard, he stuck to the glass in the evening shower.

"It's time I lost. Nothing is eternal in this world except documentation."

"What do you mean?"

"I'm giving up."

"Why?"

"I can't defeat anyone anymore. Less and less people play marbles. I've already wandered all over the world. Fewer and fewer people play marbles. Eventually there will be none."

"What is eternal in this world?"

"Only documentation."

"Yeah, yeah, yeah. Only documentation. Why don't you want to live out your fate as Marble Man? Play until death."

"Play where? I've looked everywhere. Everyone is playing Pac-Man!"

"So?"

"It's time we parted. I'm giving up."

"Where are you going?"

"To Silicon Valley."

Then, like a lizard falling, he released himself and floated down.

"Marble Maaaaannnn! Wait!"

I ran out of my office, straight to the elevator and shot downstairs. I ran through the lobby as if I was being chased by Satan and out to the parking lot. I had to save Marble Man.

But, even though I circled the building twice, I didn't find his body. I was relieved. At least he didn't die.

In the damp evening, I could hear various electronic sounds. Unnatural robotic sounds. I entered the building from where the sounds were coming. And I saw all the people in the building facing glass screens, their faces filled with tension. Not just children, but also adults, even grandparents, were there. Everyone wanted to win the game. Pac-Man had swept the world.

The creature that chomped on everything suddenly leapt through the glass screen. His body became three-dimensional and grew bigger and bigger. He broke through the room, the roof. He began wildly chewing the clouds. People were shocked. Their dream creature had become real.

"Look! It's Pac-Man!"

"Yeah, it's Pac-Man! He's become real!"

"Pac-Man! Oh, Pac-Man! Bless us! Let us experience winning! Let us experience success!"

Amazing! Those people bowed down to him and knelt forward on the floor. Their tears flowed. But Pac-Man was too busy chewing the string of rain clouds with his voracious mouth.

More and more people gathered at his feet. They started yelling.

"Long live Pac-Man!"

"Live!"

"Long live Pac-Man!"

"Live!"

I imagined Marble Man walking alone in Silicon Valley, surrendering himself to the future. He walked alone, dragging his sack, which was ripped so that the marbles rolled out one by one until they were all gone....

The Helicopter

When nine of out ten neighbors bought Mercedes Benz sedans at the same time, Saleh became upset.

"This is really too much," he said. "It seems like people don't care about the values handed down by their ancestors. Everyone's gone crazy. No one's embarrassed any more about flaunting their wealth. Apparently simplicity is no longer considered important. There is absolutely no sense of social solidarity! It's too much!"

Then he bought a Blue Thunder helicopter.

"OK," he continued, "if we're going to show off extravagance, then let's do it! Not just half way!"

The city residents, of course, went into an uproar.

"Saleh bought a helicopter!"

"What? Saleh bought a helicopter?"

"The most austere person in this city bought a helicopter?"

"Yeah. The most austere person in this city bought a helicopter!"

"His values have changed!"

"Saleh bought a helicopter? What for?"

The perfect helicopter was parked on the roof of Saleh's house. And so that it would appear even more extravagant, Saleh rarely turned off the engine. The propellers revolved continuously as if to remind everyone that it all cost a lot of money.

"We don't have to hesitate flaunting our wealth, the products of our own sweat," he told a reporter who interviewed him for the column, From Mouth to Mouth. "We're tired of being submissive. Temptation is too strong. Just imagine. Almost everyone drives a Mercedes! What for? If it's just for transportation, you don't need a Mercedes, right? It only fits four people! It's just an example of extravagance! And it's really pitiful if people pour all their arrogance into a Mercedes. Our society is in a critical situation."

"But then, why did you buy a helicopter, the most expensive vehicle in this city?"

"Because austerity is no longer important. Simplicity is too expensive. It appears that simplicity is more extravagant than luxury itself. Just be honest. Everyone wants to look great. For instance, your own camera is a Hasselblad, whereas this photo shoot is only for the column From Mouth to Mouth. Right?"

The helicopter boldly rose into the sky every morning. He hired the ace pilot, Chuck Yeager[1]. With his chin butting out over the side, he glanced at the line of Mercedes in the street. Hundreds, thousands, even hundreds of thousands of Mercedes flowed like a tributary along the length of the river. The red gathered with the red, the black with the black, the white with the white. Saleh beamed.

"Look, Chuck. This is my society. A community that is just, prosperous, *gemah ripah loh jinawi*."

"*Gemah ripah loh jinawi*? What's that? I don't understand."

---

[1]   Charles Elwood "Chuck" Yeager (born 1923) was the first pilot to (officially) fly faster than the soeed of sound (Mach 2.44) in 1947. His story is featured in the film "The Right Stuff" (directed by Philip Kaufman, 1983), which was adapted from the book of the same name by Tom Wolfe. Yeager visited the Nurtanio airplane factory in Bandung in 1985.

"Ah, you're an idiot too. It means that we are very rich!"

"Rich? Your country rich?"

"Ha ha ha ha ha ha ha! Enough, Chuck, forget it. You're just a chauffeur now. Keep driving!"

Blue Thunder flew beautifully, swerving to the left and to the right with the agility of a bird. Slipping delicately in between the high-rise buildings. Whenever office workers saw the helicopter, they would scramble to the windows. From the helicopter, Saleh could see people at the windows watching him.

"Hey, Chuck! Look at those people. They're watching us!"

"Yeah, they're looking at you, Mr. Saleh. You're a handsome guy."

"So, I'm handsome, huh, Chuck? Like a movie star! Ha ha ha ha ha ha ha ha!"

"Ha ha ha ha ha ha ha ha!"

Actually, the people were only attracted to the helicopter, which sometimes flew very low to the ground, hovering over the long line of Mercedes in the jammed streets. If Saleh felt naughty, he would order Chuck to brush up against the Mercedes. For every scratch he made, Saleh would throw a million rupiah down to the owner. The people in the Mercedes were furious.

"Arrogant!"

"Show off!"

"Just because you have a helicopter!"

"Just because we can only afford to buy a Mercedes, you don't have to be like that!"

"Even if it's only a Mercedes, we have self-respect!"

But then they took the money.

Saleh's actions were reported in the scandal sheets. His grandmother from the village felt that she had to pay him a visit.

"Saleh, my pious grandson, why have you become like this? Flaunting wealth so extravagantly?"

"What's wrong, Grandma? This is a product of my own hard work. I'm not a corrupter. I'm a business man."

"But Saleh, arrogance and waste are against religious teachings."

"Against religious teaching? Ha ha ha ha ha! Tell that to the owners of all those Mercedes."

Saleh's behavior became increasingly frivolous. He used the helicopter to go out just to buy cigarettes. Formerly Saleh had been one of the most unpretentious people in the city. He was indeed extraordinarily wealthy, but very modest. People considered him to be a model citizen, exemplary. Many people often quoted him. They had felt that anyone other than Saleh could become spoiled. He was the pillar upholding the world from disintegration. He was the embodiment of the model that promoted determination and hard work as the appropriate ways to develop the world; not to stockpile one's own wealth.

However, Saleh had now destroyed that image. One day he gathered all of his employees in a field and lectured them from his helicopter hovering above them.

"In this era, you need not be embarrassed about doing something for your own interests. Times have changed. This is the era of insanity. If you don't follow the insanity, you won't get a piece of anything. As fortunate as those who aren't insane may be, those who are insane are more fortunate. Number one is personal ambition. Number two is personal ambition. Number three is also personal ambition. Work harder for your own interests. That is the meaning of progress. Cultivate greed, selfishness, and voraciousness so you won't be left behind. Everyone must dream of owning a Mercedes. And once they achieve that, they must dream of owning a helicopter. That is the company philosophy. If you do not agree, raise your hand so that you will be fired!"

The employees, all wearing ties, were as speechless as robots. How could the upstanding Saleh speak like that? The high-principled values that Saleh formerly promoted still echoed in their ears. Saleh had always advised his employees to be more prudent. The company would advance, but many other people still needed help. These people did not have the opportunities to help themselves. This was cause for concern. We must be considerate. Our good fortune was part of other people's suffering. Don't sanction the results of your own struggle just because you have had opportunity and good fate.

Then the helicopter slowly flew off into the distance, disappearing behind the high-rise buildings. The employees returned to their own offices with questions ringing in their heads. They couldn't work. Formerly, when Saleh recommended a simple life, many of them had sneered.

"He can say that because he's filthy rich," they used to say. "Sure, he comes to work on a bicycle, but look at how wealthy he is. I bet if he were poor like us and could only buy a Mercedes, he wouldn't still dare to advise us not to dream."

"Yeah, he can say that just because he has lots of businesses. It's not as if he was concerned and paid attention to the fates of others. Just owning a Mercedes is labeled extravagant. Don't we need transportation? Don't we need to leave for work in comfort? How can we work if we're sweating even before we start? Am I right or not?"

They couldn't work. If a person as unpretentious as Saleh could change, then what would happen? Was the earth no longer habitable for good people?

"Maybe Saleh wasn't serious," they started to gossip.

"Maybe Saleh was only kidding."

"Maybe he just wanted to tease us."

"If he was teasing, then why did he use a helicopter? Explain that!"

"Probably because people are too shameless."

"If that's the case, no matter how much he teases, it won't work."

"But maybe he was serious. Maybe he's become arrogant and a show-off. He can't pretend to be modest anymore."

"Impossible."

"Yeah. It's not possible that he would change. Surely he has another purpose in mind."

"Well, that's a possibility. Why not? In a world as fragile as this one, everyone can change. Even Saleh. No one is immune. No one is beyond being influenced. We just have to accept it. Saleh has changed."

"I still don't believe it."

"I have a headache."

"Yeah, yeah. What happened to Saleh?"

In the Blue Thunder helicopter, beautiful, flawless, and agile as a bird, Saleh mused. He watched civilization growing on the asphalt. Buildings, streets, cars, people. The sun flashed and reflected.

"Light, light, what do you illuminate..." he whispered.

Sitting beside him, Chuck Yeager, who did not understand him, just piloted the helicopter. Penetrating haze, penetrating clouds, penetrating a shimmering lace of light.

"Is there still a lot of fuel, Chuck?"

"Yes, enough for three days and three nights. Where are we going?"

"Just go straight."

"Okay, boss."

How agile the helicopter was, swerving to the left and to the right as if it was dancing. Outside the city, farmers waved to them from the rice fields. Saleh blinked as he watched buffaloes dragging plows. When he was young, he enjoyed tending his buffalo in the grassy fields. He liked to ride his buffalo while playing his bamboo flute. How happy he had been. The helicopter kept flying onward. The propellers rotated magnificently, stirring pride in its passenger. They reached the ocean. Saleh saw the long white line of the waves breaking. He saw fishing boats and an occasional flying fish.

Saleh smiled.

"Go lower, Chuck. I want to smell the ocean."

Chuck lowered Blue Thunder. The ocean water parted under the roar of the propellers. Saleh opened the doors. He took a deep breath.

"Do you smell that, Chuck?"

"What?"

"The ocean!"

"Yeah!"

"Refreshing, isn't it, Chuck?"

"Salty!"

"I said, refreshing, Chuck! Say 'refreshing'!"

"Okay, okay! Refreshing!"

"Good. Go on!"

The helicopter kept going, penetrating clouds, penetrating haze, penetrating shimmering light. The sound of the engine reverberated, stirring the webs of his thoughts, the threads of temptation, extracting complexities and considerations. The helicopter flew through blood cells, swept through arteries and floated freely in the network of the brain. They were surrounded by blackness. Chuck turned on all the lights. But the blackness persisted and the shining lights did not strike anything. To Chuck Yeager it felt as if they had been flying in the darkness for a thousand years.

"Don't do anything fancy. This helicopter is flying through your thoughts. We have to return to the real world!"

"OK, OK. Fly to the real world."

"How? The navigational equipment isn't working anymore."

"Keep going."

The helicopter flew on, free of the darkness, enveloped by blue sky. Chuck Yeager wiped the cold sweat from his forehead. The air was refreshing. They were flying over a jungle.

"Where are we, Chuck?"

"I don't know. Most of the equipment isn't functioning anymore. Is doesn't feel like we're flying over earth."

"Which jungle is this, Chuck? Kalimantan?"

"No, Kalimantan's forest is gone."

"So, which forest is this? Where have we strayed to?"

"If I knew, I would have already told you, Mister."

The helicopter was still flying through the blue sky, which had become gray and cloudy. Saleh glanced down. The wild jungle stretched out like a vast green carpet. The sky was motionless. There was haze everywhere. The sound of the engines reverberated, rebounding in the valleys, off cliffs, and through canyons.

Suddenly, beyond the sound of the engine, they could hear a heavy flapping of wings. A dark shadow passed the helicopter. Chuck Yeager was startled.

"Shit! A gigantic bird!"

"What, Chuck?"

"Look!" Chuck pointed.

"Are there birds like that in Indonesia? This is really dangerous for airplanes!"

Saleh saw the bird that was flapping heavily and flying quickly into the distance. Actually, it wasn't flying, it was soaring. It reminded Saleh of something.

"Chuck, look in the Blue Thunder computer. I want to know what kind of bird that is."

Chuck's fingers danced on the keyboard. He shook his head.

"It's not a bird. It's a prehistoric flier—a pterosaur!"

"What?!"

"Yes, look! It's from the Jurassic Era!"

"Oh God, Chuck. Where are we?"

"I don't know, Mister. Argh! Look down there!"

"Oh my God! It's the head of a brontosaurus!"

Chuck pointed again.

"Look! Look! Look!"

"Oh, God! Allosaurus is fighting stegosaurus!"

This is indeed what Saleh and Chuck Yeager saw. Brontosaurus heads emerged out of the dense jungle. A volcano billowed forth ash clouds. Cetiosaurus, ceratosaurus, ornitholestes dinosaurs were everywhere. Frightening, gigantic prehistoric animals. Their mouths gaping open, searching for prey; a world that seemed like hell. No humanity. Quiet. Desolate. Only wild dense jungle.

Saleh's eyes were glassy.

"Chuck, we have to get away from here! I want to go home!"

"Where else is there to go? We're still on earth!"

"But this isn't our earth!"

"No, this is indeed our earth!"

"Our earth is filled with humans, not prehistoric creatures!"

"Whatever it's filled with, this is definitely our earth. The computer shows it that that is where we are!"

Saleh's tears flowed.

"Sir! The fuel is almost gone! There's no place to land! What should we do?"

"Keep going!"

The helicopter flew through the mist, its sound reverberating, shattering the prehistoric silence.

"Sir! There's only three minutes left! We have to land or we'll crash and be destroyed!"

"Keep going!"

The long neck of the brontosaurus stretched up to the sky. The helicopter began to wobble unsteadily. Saleh screamed hysterically, his tears flowed down his cheeks.

"What is all this progress for, God, if we are still the same as prehistoric creatures?! Yes, we're greedy! Yes, we only think of our own stomachs! But we're humans, aren't we?! Are You teasing me, God? I'm offended! I—"

"Sir! We're out of fuel! We're crashing!"

The helicopter propellers stopped. Blue Thunder inverted into a nose dive. There was no engine noise. Only silence. Only Saleh screaming.

"God! So we are still living in the prehistoric period!!"

Rrrrrr ...

The next day, the people in the city felt something was missing. The day after that the scandal sheets irresponsibly reported Saleh's disappearance:

INDUSTRIALIST SALEH KIDNAPPED BY RED BRIGADES!

The Ticket Counter

It was still early. A cardboard sign hung in the ticket counter window: CLOSED. Inside were a jacket hanging on the back of a chair, a stack of brand new tickets, and stamps scattered on the table. A poster calendar featuring a beautiful smiling woman was tacked up on the wall. A neon light shone brightly.

People started to line up. An elderly man was in the front. In fact, he was at the counter when it was still dark. He arrived just past midnight, spread out a mat under the counter and slept there. He woke up very early in the morning, ate some food he had brought, then stood in front of the ticket counter. He knew that the ticket agent had arrived. The agent had thrown his jacket onto the chair and then gone out again. Perhaps he went out to the restroom.

A woman in an official uniform stood behind the old man. A young man who looked like a university student was behind her reading a newspaper. Behind him there was a soldier wearing a red beret and a commando knife at his waist. Then, there was a *haji* wearing a sarong and carrying a plastic bag. There was a young man with a camera hanging from his neck. There was a young woman carrying her baby in a shoulder sling. There was a man who looked like a messenger. There was a man wearing a fez. There was someone without shoes. There was a man who looked like a transvestite. There was a young person wearing a school uniform.

There was a woman wearing the traditional Javanese women's long-sleeve blouse and a batik wrap-around skirt. There was someone who, it seemed, had not taken a bath. There was a very sweet girl wearing a head veil.

Someone in the back of the line looked at his watch.

"It should be open already. Where's the agent? Why isn't he around?" he yelled impatiently.

"Yeah, where is the guy? I'm already late!" commented someone else.

Other people looked back.

"Patience, *Pak*! It's still early!"

"Sure it's still early, but it should be open by now!"

"Yeah, yeah. It should be open. But, you know, they're usually late here."

The person who had yelled didn't reply even though he was pouting. Someone else shouted out from the back.

"*Pak*! You, in the front! Has the agent arrived or not?"

"Yes, he's here!"

"Where is he now?"

"He said he was going out for a bit!"

"Where?"

"I don't know! Maybe to the restroom!"

Hearing this, the people in the back started to calm down, but there were still some complaints.

"Why is he taking so long in the bathroom?"

"Stomach ache maybe."

"He works only when he wants to, maybe."

"Don't say that. He's just a low-ranking employee; his pay is low."

"Even if his pay is low, he still has responsibilities!"

"Ah, that's enough. The counter will open eventually. He's already here."

People kept coming. The line grew longer. A security guard appeared out of who knows where and straightened out the line that was beginning to go astray.

"Sir, sir, please, sir, try to be orderly. Ma'am, ma'am, behind the man here. Yes, yes, be patient. Yes, everyone will get a chance. Hey, can you be orderly or not? If I roughen you up, maybe then you'll learn your lesson!"

The security guard's eyes widened when he spotted a young man with a ponytail who was sitting on the floor, smoking. Lazily, the young man stood up and pretended to look elsewhere.

Newspaper vendors, cigarette sellers, shoe shiners, even bottled drink vendors began to mill around the line. There were people selling candy, fans, even porno pictures. The people in line who were beginning to get bored started to casually buy whatever was offered. Shoes were slipped off, people munched while they filled in crossword puzzles. The place was getting littered. Leaf wrappings for tofu, plastic bags, peanut shells, boxes, and cigarette butts scattered about, bumping against the empty bottles, which were unintentionally kicked around.

Those who arrived late did not know the line was not yet moving. They stood at the end of the line and read newspapers or stared into space with their hands in their pockets. Their faces were blank and dumb. Suddenly, a woman screamed.

"Help! Pickpocket! *Help!*"

She seemed to point towards someone. The line dispersed immediately. The accused person was quickly surrounded. His face was drained and his mouth trembled.

"It's not me, sir! Not me!"

But his voice was lost under the sound of punches, kicks and the blows of hard objects beating his body. He was soundly thrashed. Faces that had been blank and dumb were now wild and hungry for blood. Everyone wanted to contribute to his torture.

"Have mercy, sir! Have mercy!"

The assault went on. Lumps appeared on his head, his face became swollen until it was shapeless and blood flowed from his nose and mouth. He grimaced, showing reddened teeth.

Fortunately, the security guard arrived before it got any worse. He blew his whistle and he struggled through the violent crowd.

"What is this?! Taking the law in your own hands! Break it up! Get back!"

He struck out with his rubber club so the crowd dispersed, leaving the man sprawled out on the floor in a pitiful condition. Furious, the security guard stood with his arms on his hips.

"Dogs! Creating havoc! Can't you be a little orderly? Insolence! I treat you politely, and you act like animals!"

People were dumb-founded. They appeared to be too lazy to obey the security guard. They seemed to be satisfied just to have been able to release some emotion.

"Come on! Get in line again! In the exact same order!"

And they returned to the line as before. Their faces became blank and dumb again. Several people had returned to the crossword puzzles they had abandoned. A young man stuck his Walkman earphones back into his ears. The bottled tea hawkers struck their bottles with the bottle cap openers.

"I swear, sir! I'm not the pickpocket! I don't know anything!" pleaded the crying man, his mouth full of blood.

"Enough! We'll go to the police station right now!" snapped the security guard and began dragging the victim of the crowd's rage.

"*Pak! Pak!* What about my money, *Pak?*" interrupted the woman who claimed her wallet was stolen. She grasped the arm of the guard. The three of them vanished behind the gateway.

It was mid-morning. The line grew longer. The end of the line reached far out into the building's courtyard. It curved around the fence. The line stretched out like a snake along the length of the street.

The day grew hotter. People were busy fanning themselves. Perspiration dotted their faces. The backs of their shirts became damp with sweat. Several of them shamelessly began to unbutton their shirts. Fragrant handy-wipe towelettes were in demand. Its aroma pierced the stuffiness. Several sleepy people were scattered throughout the line. The ticket counter still hadn't opened.

The people who had arrived early became impatient again. They asked the security guard who was pacing back and forth while striking his rubber club in his palm.

"Hey, *Mas*! Where's the agent? We've been waiting since this morning!"

"Yeah! What's going on? Is the counter going to open or not?"

"Don't play with us!"

"Don't play around!"

"Give us an answer!"

"Time is money these days, *Mas*!"

The security guard stared.

"Hey! Don't ask me! I'm only the security guard! I don't know anything! Ask the man in the front of the line. He knows where the agent went."

The elderly man in the front of the line was asleep standing up. His face was buried in his two folded arms, which were leaning against the counter. Everyone looked at him.

"Oh no! He's sleeping!"

"Just wake him up!"

"No! Poor thing! He's old!"

"But he's the only person who knows. What did he say?"

"What was it? I forgot. It was earlier this morning!"

"Come on, ask him again! Just wake him up! This is in the interests of many people!"

"That's right! In the interests of many people! If he wants to sleep, he shouldn't sleep here!"

The old man continued to snore. Who knows what he was dreaming. The woman in the uniform tapped his back.

"*Pak, Pak*, wake up! These people want to ask you something."

But he continued to snore. Apparently, he was very tired. People were increasingly impatient.

"Just splash water on him!"

"Sssst! Don't do that! He's an old man!"

"Well then, shake him. Don't just tap his shoulder. That'll just make him sleep more soundly."

"*Pak! Pak!* Wake up, *Pak!* It's already noon!"

The security guard also joined in rousing him. He nudged the old man's hand.

"What did the ticket agent say, *Pak?*"

"He said he was going out briefly," said the old man with a sleepy voice.

"Where?"

"He didn't say. Maybe to the back."

"Back! Back where? The restroom? To pee?"

"I don't know. He didn't say."

"Shit! What is it? Speak clearly!"

"That's all I know. Enough. Now I'm going to sleep again, OK? I'm sleepy. Later, when he comes, please wake me up. Don't forget," he said again. Then he was snoring. People shook their heads.

"Old geezer! He's senile. Poor thing."

"But that's all he knows. He said the same thing this morning. He arrived the earliest. He's the only witness."

"So, what now?"

"Yeah, what?"

Slowly, people began looking towards the security guard. He felt uncomfortable.

"Hey, hey, don't do that. I'm only an employee," he said, retreating.

Someone leapt forward and grabbed the collar of the guard's shirt.

"Don't just take it easy, OK? You're the only employee here. Don't just pick on the kids. You go around carrying a club. When a serious problem comes around you want to bark, but you can't! Go and look for the guy! Now! We can't wait forever. We have important matters to tend to. Look for the guy! Quickly!"

"Oh, no, *Pak!* Have mercy, *Pak!* Where should I look?" His voice trembled. Now he appeared to be a coward.

"Didn't you hear what the man said? Look for him in the restroom! Who knows, maybe he's sick in there."

"Yeah. Quick, look for him! We need to know!"

The guard disappeared. The people returned to the line. In the same order. It was hot and people fanned themselves continuously. Child vendors of ice popsicles, soft drinks, plastic bags of tea, and ice fruit cocktail appeared. They were mobbed until they sold everything they had. More litter was scattered about. Flies buzzed.

The security guard returned. "He's not in the back, *Pak!*"

"Where did you go?"

"To the restroom, *Pak!*"

"Imbecile! Idiot! Does 'going to the back' have to mean just 'going to the restroom'?"

"What else would it mean, *Pak?*"

"Dummy! What else can 'going to the back' mean here? You're the one who should know!"

He disappeared again. The people stood in line and grumbled. The line got longer, twisting along the sidewalk. It was no longer clear where the tail was.

Newcomers asked those in the front: "The counter isn't open yet, is it?"

"Not yet."

"As late as this?"

"So it seems. They said the agent just went out for a while."

"Where?"

"They said maybe to the restroom."

"Ohhhh…"

The security guard appeared in the front again.

"He's not there, *Pak*. I've looked everywhere. He's not at the food stall, the cigarette stand, the billiard parlor, the market, or even in the massage parlor, *Pak*."

"Look at his home!"

"Ah, I don't know where he lives, *Pak!*"

"Then ask! There has to be someone who knows!"

"Dead end! There isn't anyone who knows, *Pak!* No one around here knows each other's houses. We never mix in personal matters, *Pak!* We only know each other professionally!"

The people were silent. They did not demand anymore. They also knew there wasn't anyone who took care of their personal affairs. But they still had hope. Someone again asked the old man in the front.

"*Pak! Pak!* He said he was just going outside for a while, right, *Pak?*"

The old man did not answer. His position was still the same. His face was buried in his folded arms on the ticket counter. It seemed as if he was still asleep.

"Enough. Don't bother him. Poor thing. Old man."

"Look, the problem is we have to know whether the guy is coming back again!"

"That's true. If that's the case, quick ask again!"

Someone approached the old man and tapped his shoulder.

"*Pak, Pak*. Wake up a minute, *Pak*. We need to know."

But the old man was as stiff as a statue.

"Just tap his shoulder, then he'll wake up for sure."

They pushed the old man who then fell over like a banana tree that had been chopped down. The woman in official uniform behind him screamed. People crowded around. The old man was laid out to full length. He didn't move at all.

"Wow, maybe he's dead."

Several people tried to examine him. Someone pushed open his eyelids, someone tried to take his pulse by holding his wrist, someone listened to his chest. Someone passed smelling salts under his nose, someone placed a damp towel on his forehead.

"How is he? Is he still alive?"

"His heart is still beating."

"That's a sign he's still alive."

"But he can't move."

"That's okay, at least he's still alive."

"Indeed, but he can't answer our question. We need to know."

"Whatever it is, it's better than dying. If he's still alive, he might still be able to answer our question. If he dies, then there's absolutely no hope."

"It looks as if he's dead. He's still alive, but can't do anything. Actually, he's virtually dead."

"But not yet, right? His heart is still beating, right? There's still hope."

"What hope? We need a definite answer!"

"Aaaghhh! What's definite in this world?"

People continued to debate and the old man just lay there. His body was laid out like a corpse. The flies started to gather around parts of his body.

"So what should we do? The only witness cannot answer."

"Hey, what did he say?"

"He said that the agent was going out for a little while. Maybe to the back."

"He said just for a while, right?"

"Yeah."

"He said to the back, right?"

"Maybe."

"Yeah, but he is coming back, isn't he?"

"Yeah, he's supposed to. That's his jacket still on the chair."

"So, yeah, we'll just wait."

"What?! What if he doesn't came back? How long do we wait? The time is already too close. We must hurry. We have to get the tickets. We can't not get them."

"He said he was going out for only a while, right?"

It was night. The line was still getting longer. The old man's body was dragged over to the side and just left to lie there. Abandoned in a swarm of flies. There was no one who knew for certain, and no one who wanted to know, whether he was still alive or not.

Several people spread out newspapers and went to sleep in line. Several people played cards or chess. There were also those who daydreamed or watched other people. People stayed in their own places in line, in the same order. The woman in uniform replaced the old man at the head of the line. Everyone took one step forward.

The line became longer. It twisted and turned the length of the city. People kept coming. They joined the line in an orderly fashion. Those who were sleepy went to sleep sitting up or spread out newspapers in place. Night dew moistened their tired faces. Snores were heard here and there, but there were still people standing in line in several places. Their faces were dull, hazy, and exhausted, but still appeared to harbor hope.

The night vendors appeared. Sellers of roasted corn, steamed cakes, boiled peanuts, steamed buns, omelets, fried bananas, and ginger tea, as well as blind masseurs shadowed the line while continuously sounding their own characteristic calls. The faces of the vendors also seemed less than energetic. It was as if they were only carrying out their daily duties for minimal profit. As long as it was enough to eat, enough to continue living, enough to survive.

A night of darkness. Night, gloomy in a choking polluted haze. Several people in line conversed quietly, whispering because they were afraid of disturbing others. Minutes crept by. The earth continued to revolve. Turn. Stars blinked gloomily in the distant sky. Distant sky. Life and dreams interwoven in obscurity. Obscurity. Life was like a dream. Like a dream.

The line grew longer. People slept, exhausted. People whispered.

"*Mas, mas*, has the agent arrived?"

"Not yet."

"Tomorrow morning he'll come for sure, right? Tomorrow the counter will be open, won't it?"

"They said he only went to the back. For a little while."

"So there's still a possibility the counter will open, right?"

"Yes, still possible."

So it was, people slept with assurance that it was still possible that the ticket counter would open. Time passed. Days later, weeks later, months later, years later, the line still grew longer. The person at the end of the line no longer knew where the line began.

The people waiting in line grew older. Their beards and moustaches grew longer. Many of them died there. Those who died were then shoved to the side so that those in the back could move forward. The scattered corpses began to decay. Many had only bones left even though the clothes were intact. Flies swarmed. Trash piled up. But they still stood in an orderly line. Occasionally, events occurred that disturbed the line, but those moments passed quickly and were forgotten. People keeled over and died, and new people arrived. The security guard had grown old and absent-minded; trembling and weak, he remained on guard duty.

The light was bright. A cardboard sign hung in back of the counter window: CLOSED. A jacket hugging the back of a chair, a pile of tickets not yet used, and rubber stamps scattered about were visible inside the ticket room. A calendar poster featuring a beautiful smiling woman was posted on a wall. A neon lamp shone dimly, fluttering as if close to expiring. Someone at the end of the line asked the person in front of him: "*Mas, mas,* is the ticket counter open yet?"

Whose Baby is Crying
in the Bushes?

The morning, moist with dew, was pierced by the wailing of a baby. I rushed towards the bushes near the ditch and my universe was immediately shaken. The dew-moist morning, hazy with splinters of sunshine peeking between the bamboo leaves, was soaked with blood that streamed into the membranes of my vision. A blood-red world. In front of me was a newborn baby, blood-smeared and screaming, surrounded by a pack of dogs that were barking incessantly. The baby was lying in the middle of a heap of trash, which was a mess because of the dogs scrambling over each other for the baby. Garbage of dry leaves, food scraps, plastic, rags, and rat carcasses. The dogs' snouts, grimacing with red tongues hanging out and saliva dripping. Their barks pounded in my ears as if they were the loudest sounds in the world with the baby's cries punctuating the barks, as if the dogs had pounced on him. My God, a baby born just five minutes ago. Whose baby was it?

I imagined a woman sprawled out on top of the garbage heap in the middle of the night, clutching her heaving belly tightly. Her face damp with perspiration, her body drenched, her hair wet, and her clothes rumpled. Her odor, mixed with the stench of the trash, seeping into her suffering. Rolling back and forth with long moans, which she tried to suppress so that no one would hear: "Aaaaoooowwwwwww…"

Her legs spread apart, her skirt parted. In such a condition she was totally repellent to all, except those who were truly lust-starved and could not pay the cheapest, most degraded prostitute. Surely, the woman was emotionally unfit; surely she was totally unaware of herself; surely she did not know that she was pregnant with an innocent baby, an ill-fated child who was now crying, screaming frantically because creatures called dogs were barking at it and even had begun to lick the baby's skin lightly. The dogs had not bitten the baby because they were fighting amongst themselves for the victor who would dominate. The dogs fought and scrapped with each other; every dog sought a chance to sink it's sharp teeth into the soft baby skin as a sign of possession, but whenever one of them approached the baby, another one would attack it, so chaos reigned. The baby continued to scream even though it was not certain whether he knew fear was.

Where was his mother? Perhaps his mother was a cheap hooker who had no feelings, who gave birth to the baby while squatting, as if she was urinating, and just left it in the drainage ditch after cleaning herself up. Perhaps she did this with every baby she became pregnant with because her body was, indeed, only an object to make money with for her own survival. A baby would bring incredible complications to her life. Of course, she was not the only woman who did this, because there were many stories in the newspapers that reported babies had been found in trash containers, rivers, sacks, in the middle of rice fields, or the tiger's cage at the zoo. It was incomprehensible.

The barking increased. One dog was badly wounded, its stomach ripped open and its ear almost torn off by another dog. Its blood splattered the screaming baby. It also splattered the faces of the other dogs so that they looked like creatures sent from hell to shatter the peaceful morning in the village on the edge of the city when the earth was still damp and the sunrays shimmered from behind the bamboo cluster. I watched the event unfold through a disoriented timeframe.

The world was splashed with red blood. A dog sunk his teeth into the baby's thigh and the baby's cry, which was already at a high volume, rose several octaves higher, shrieking up to the sky. Fortunately, the puncture was brief because other dogs attacked the dog. The bite marks were visible on the baby's leg. Blood red.

Perhaps the baby's mother was not a prostitute or a crazy person or even a cheap slut. Perhaps she was a high-class woman, refined, sincere, soft-spoken, and sensible in everyday life, but someone who had fallen madly in love with a young, spiteful scoundrel who ended up breaking her heart, even infecting her with a venereal disease that made her desperate so that she could not sacrifice her personal life for the baby because her husband was a famous, respected community figure, nationally praised. And, what would people say if a refined woman, the wife of a sluggish official, gave birth to someone else's baby when her own husband never slept with her?

So, when the baby was born secretly in a hidden place with the help of loyal servants, the baby was quickly bundled up. Then he was carefully secreted away for a ride on a horse cart, which had been waiting, and then spurred on to the edge of the city where the baby was still screaming, his face making us weep.

The morning had been quiet because there had been an all-night shadow puppet performance held for the safety and welfare of the entire village. During the past several years, the villagers' rice fields had suffered bad harvests and, who knows why, several villagers had died unnaturally, that is, by suicide. Some had hung themselves, others drank insecticide and others threw themselves in front of approaching trains.

The shadow puppet play featuring the story *Murwakala* seemed to captivate all of the villagers so they were able to stay up all night. Now they did not really care about the barking dogs fighting over a newborn baby squirming by himself amidst the garbage at the edge of the drainage canal and crying shrilly because a pack of dogs surrounded him and were barking at him, perhaps even going to eat him.

I was still frozen in place, only half-conscious, gazing at the baby. Five or six dogs surrounded the newborn baby who continued to cry shrilly—but strangely, none of them bit him. Not long after that, more dogs arrived. Seven, ten, fifteen, twenty, twenty-five... Perhaps news had spread amongst the dogs that there was a delicious meal in the middle of the bushes at the edge of the drainage ditch on a chilly, quiet morning like this. And the especially delicious meal was a human child, mmm.... If the humans had thrown away this soft meat in the bushes filled with trash, didn't that mean that they had given it up as a meal for us, who were always given the scraps, except when we were able to scavenge for ourselves in the garbage, like now?

My God, who would have the heart to throw away this baby five minutes ago? How could something like this happen? How could she throw away this baby? Perhaps she kissed it tenderly first, gazed at it with glassy eyes, then said:

"Oh, my child, my sweetheart, my darling. Look at you; you resemble your father. We must part now, my darling, apple of my eye, diamond of my heart, pearl of my eternal love. This really is not what I want, my dear child, but, oh, what can I do? I'm a weak, powerless woman? I shall carry this sin no matter how heavy it is, to guard the name of my family, oh my poor, loved child. Why must I discard you..."

Perhaps the woman carefully placed the baby down in the cleanest spot in the middle of the bushes at the edge of the drainage ditch and she left with tears flowing and now who knows what she was doing. Perhaps she was now sleeping next to her husband in this very village. How beautiful the woman was, but how weak of heart. Of course, I didn't know what really happened. Whose child had been thrown away? Was this a child of an illicit relationship with a young neighbor? A child of her own husband, unwanted because she could not support it? Had she been afraid of aborting the pregnancy?

The world was red with the blood that streamed down from the sky. Red wherever the eye could see—red earth, red trash, red baby, red dogs, red leaves, red bamboo shoots, red shimmering sunrays, and red blood draining down from the sky, very slowly. Slowly, gracefully, but sure to drown us in blood, blood, blood, blood, and blood....

Whose baby lay sprawled in the bushes surrounded by twenty-five wild dogs that were, very possibly, going to rip him apart shortly and run away dragging his intestines along the village streets and, in the blink of an eye, would be devoured, leaving only the bones which would probably be eaten too because they were soft and the dogs were ravenous? Worthless mongrels, mangy dogs covered with sores.

I watched the horrifying scene unfold. I seemed to be watching one thousand years go by without being able to blink. What events had brought this baby here now? Was he an illegitimate child of a prince or market racketeer? Had a prince made love with the queen or had the market racketeer raped the herbal drink seller or had a cheap hooker thrown him away as she often did because no man would acknowledge the child as his own and even she didn't feel a need to take care of it?

Whose child was this? The seed of a father from a grandfather from a great grandfather, sprinting from spirit to spirit, from century to century, from a major dynasty, from a life story, from a legend. Heaven forbid, would the fairy tale end in the mouths of twenty-five dogs?

The morning was cool and quiet. A caterpillar crawled on a leaf as dew dripped and the world shifted and the temperature rose ever so slightly and the wind changed directions and yellow butterflies fluttered over the trash and many of the ants under the baby died. A dog too had died of blood loss after being attacked by the other dogs.

The baby's umbilical cord had been cut, hanging limply, dirty because the placenta had been dragged through the dirt. The baby was now filthy. His mouth had been stuck to a margarine can that had fallen away, but left a wound. His mouth was torn slightly; his tears trickled down pitifully. A dog had bitten one of his arms and was pulling the baby to the edge of the ditch. The other dogs scrambled to attack that dog. It backed down, cowering. Five dogs fought on his back while barking wildly, greedily, ruthlessly, voraciously.

Did his mother throw her past away? She was someone who came from far away. She traveled all night to this place. A place she had known very well since her childhood. She had hidden somewhere for nine months and at the right time she crossed over to the island by ship then transferred to a night bus, then continued on by *becak* and then in the clear, dew-filled morning, she lay down in the bushes. She tossed this way and that while moaning and begging for God's mercy and begging for forgiveness for her sins. She considered all of this as a required role she had to play, like the prophet Abraham who, without hesitation, was willing to sacrifice Ishmael fulfilling God's command.

When the baby's head emerged, they looked at each other. What stuck in the baby's mind when he saw his mother giving birth in a place as rotten as this? What was recorded in the baby's brain after he came out of his mother's womb and the woman wept convulsively? And the woman would hold the baby lovingly and feed him while weeping. And when the tears stopped, he could hear a sweet lullaby floating in the chilly morning air, weaving between the sunrays that were emerging from behind the bamboo cluster.

A sad song about futile love. A song of yearning, deep, poignant, and full of longing, but not pleading. Words that moved the heart to pity, completely crushing the soul. That morning was so still while everyone slept soundly, even though the sun had already risen, so the natural breath of the morning had a chance to whisper without being bothered by civilization that polluted the earth. Tips of flower buds trembled, catching the howling wind, quiet sounds behind the soft swishing of the water flowing slowly through the canal.

Heaven forbid, the dogs again, saw the action in slow motion. The dogs' movements were like a dance. They pulled at each other with their mouths filled with sharp teeth, not false ones; glistening white teeth turned red with each other's blood. One dog lost his tail. Some dogs limped, some lost parts of their noses, some lost sight in both eyes. They fought amongst themselves and every dog tried for the first chance to bite the baby, but there was always another dog that held him back. The baby screamed hysterically, shaking his body and soul.

Oh God, the dogs' barks worsened. The dogs were fighting over the baby. One dog bit his hand, pulled, and ripped the baby's arm off because another dog had bitten the other arm. Ah, the baby was formless mess, destroyed by the pack of dogs. One dog ran here and there carrying an arm in his mouth, another carried a leg, others fought over the intestines, which had spilled and stretched out because they were pulled back and forth, and there was one that ran away with it and around in circles, chased by the others. Each claimed a portion to swallow; the baby was shredded into pieces of fresh red meat that glistened in the cold, quiet morning in a village on the edge of town....

My eyes were tired from watching this journey of one thousand years. The horrifying scene transformed my view of this world. I was still standing, watching the final vicious scene, unimaginable in my dreams. I had entered a nightmare. I wanted to close my eyes, but they were so heavy. For a thousand years, I was held prisoner by that wild scene, denied permission to close my eyes for even one second. The sun melted into a puddle of blood. The sky drained itself, becoming a river of red blood that overflowed in threateningly slow motion. Oh, my world, a flood of blood.

I was drowning in a dark sea of blood. Choked by the flood, I couldn't breathe. Floating between life and death in the midst of blood, bubbling like mud in a crater. It seemed as if my heart stopped and my lungs burst. I was surrounded by darkness, my eyes blocked by a stinking pool of blood. I struggled to glance to the side; it was so heavy, as if I had to lift a one hundred-ton steel iron sheet as if it was a thin shield. But I was shocked when I succeeded.

The baby was still there and the dogs were there too, as they were the first time I saw them. He did indeed cry in the beginning, but then stopped and, instead, he laughed and his hands moved as if signaling the dogs to play. How handsome and chubby the baby was. His face emitted a dazzling radiance and the dogs seemed not to be beasts, but noble, pleasing creatures.

This was a world exalted by a song of the skies that could not be sung. A world glistening and lofty, enlightened by a divine radiance. Oh heavens! How easily my perspective changed. The baby was giggling with his small sweet mouth, his face so pure and brave, and he seemed determined to play with the dogs. The bushes around him shimmered now, not just from the reflecting sunrays. The trash had lost its stench and became fragrant. The air was full of silvery sparkles, as if there were a thousand suns shining on this spot. I felt embarrassed to be wearing only my sarong and T-shirt on this glorious morning.

The world was radiant. Every object glistened like a jewel when illuminated. It rained crystals on the world and every granule of dirt sparkled like diamond dust. In this game of light, the baby was sometimes visible and sometimes not. Between brief glimpses, I could see the baby moving and the twenty-five dogs around it did not appear like dogs. My heart pounded in anticipation and imagination. Who placed this baby in these bushes?

Was his mother a cheap hooker or an angel? The baby's eyes were innocent, but humbling; his cheerful face was pleasant, but made one tremble; and his eyes looked sharply up while laughing with assurance and a bit of mocking mixed with amusement over his birth in this world. I squinted, trying to see the baby more clearly, but it was in vain. Sometimes visible, sometimes not, I could see only an image that touched me deeply. My body started to sweat and tremble.

I almost began to sob wholeheartedly, but I restrained myself because I didn't want to get carried away. I still could not erase the feeling that I had just woken up from a long sleep and was startled to see this baby crying shrilly in the bushes near the drainage ditch, encircled by the village dogs. Oh, God, a baby still smeared with blood, with its placenta and umbilical cord, that appeared to have been born just five minutes ago....

Glossary

bajaj	A three-wheeled passenger vehicle with a noisy pull-start motor.
becak	A tricycle pedicab which is used for passenger transport throughout Indonesia.
dangdut	Popular grassroots music marked by a strong beat (*tik-tik-ndang-ndut*), influenced by Indian and Malay music.
gemah ripah loh jinawi	Javanese, literary phrase used to describe a prosperous, flourishing, fertile country.
haji	A male Muslim who has made the holy pilgrimage (*haj*) to Mecca and Medina.
jaipongan	Popular music and dance style which originated in West Java.
keris	Javanese and Balinese ceremonial dagger with double-edged serpentine blade.
keroncong	Popular music influenced by Portuguese and Malay music; usually employs violin, cello, bass, ukelele, mandolin, flute; appeals to the elder generation.
kliwon	Fifth day of the five-day Javanese market week. The calendar runs alongside the conventional seven day week, thus each day is a conjunction of the two complimentary calendrical cycles, e.g. Monday Kliwon.
lebaran	End of the fasting month.
legi	First day of the five-day Javanese market week.
lurah	Village headman.

martabak	Omelette a la India, meat and vegetable filling wrapped in a thin egg batter and pan-fried, served hot.
mas	Term of address, derives from Javanese *kangmas*; lit. "older brother", used for any male of approximate equal age to the speaker.
mbak	Term of address, derives from Javanese *mbakyu*; lit. "older sister", used for any female of approximate equal age to the speaker.
paing	Second day of the five-day Javanese market week. (Also "*pahing*.")
pak	Term of address, derives from Indonesian *bapak*; literally "father," used for any older male or one to whom the speaker must show respect (government official, teacher, etc.).
pon	Third day of the five-day Javanese market week.
R.T.	Abbreviation of "*Rukun Tetangga,*" a neighborhood association, the lowest administrative unit.
selamatan	Ritual communal meal marking significant life cycle events or acts of thanksgiving.
semakin	Literally "increasing."
tahu guling	Diced tofu mixed with tempe or soybean curd, bean sprouts and shredded cabbage, served with sweet spicy soy sauce.
tempé	Protein-rich cake of fermented soybeans, a staple of the Indonesian diet; cooked in a variety of ways.
wagé	Fourth day of the five-day Javanese market week.
walang kèkèk	A kind of beetle but, in this instance, the title of a popular keroncong song.

Publication History

All titles in this collection were published in *Penembak Misterius: Kumpulan Cerita Pendek*. Jakarta: Pustaka Utama Grafiti, 1993. First publication dates for the stories are shown in the table below.

English Title	Indonesian Title	First Published
The Keroncong Killing	Keroncong Pembunuhan	*Kompas*, February 3, 1985
The Sound of Rain on the Roof	Bunyi Hujan di atas Genting	*Kompas*, July 28, 1985
Grrrh!	Grrh!	*Kompas*, January 18, 1987
Sarman	Sarman	*Kompas*, January 19, 1986
The Last Becak in the World (or Rambo)	Becak Terakhir di Dunia (atawa Rambo)	*Kompas*, March 23, 1986
The Potted Jasmine Plant	Melati dalam Pot	*Kompas*, May 4, 1986
Two Small Children	Dua Anak Kecil	*Kompas*, September 1986
The Tragedy of Asih, Wife of Sukab	Tragedi Asih Istrinya Sukab	*Kompas*, March 29, 1987
The Woman at the Bus Stop	Seorang Wanita di Halte Bis	*Kompas*, December 20, 1987
Semangkin (formerly Semakin)	Semangkin (d/h Semakin)	previously unpublished
The Sun	Srengenge	*Kompas*, November 2, 1986

English Title	Indonesian Title	First Published
Marble Man	Manusia Gundu	*Kompas*, March 13, 1988
Helicopter	Helikopter	*Kompas*, May 29, 1988
The Ticket Counter	Loket	*Suara Pembaruan*, March 11, 1990
Whose Baby is Crying in the Bushes?	Bayi Siapa Menangis di Semak-semak?	*Zaman*, September 29, 1984

Biographical Information

Seno Gumira Ajidarma, author of more than 30 books of short stories, essays, journalism, novels, graphic novels and plays, is one of Indonesia's most distinctive and influential voices. His range is immense, from comic urban sketches to the searing prose of *Eyewitness,* which along with *Jazz, Perfume and the Incident* confronts the New Order government's treatment of East Timor.

Born in Boston in 1958, son of a faculty member of the Gadjah Mada University in Yogyakarta, Seno rebelled early against formal schooling and, between junior and senior high school, ran away from his home in Java to work briefly in a Sumatran *krupuk* (shrimp cracker) factory. On his return he became involved in experimental theater and began writing. He published his first poem in *Horison* at the age of 18. Later he completed an undergraduate degree in cinematography and graduate degrees in philosophy and literature even while contributing regularly to newspapers and magazines.

Among his numerous literary prizes are the Southeast Asia Write award (1997), multiple Khatulistiwa (Equator) Literary Awards (2004, 2005), the Pena Kencana (Golden Pen) Award (2008) and several Best Short Story of the Year awards from the national newspaper *Kompas,* most recently in 2010.

JOAN SUYENAGA was born and raised in Honolulu, Hawaii, and earned an MA in anthropology from the University of Hawaii. She began studying traditional Javanese gamelan music and language in the early 1970s, and has lived, raised a family, and worked in Yogyakarta as a freelance writer, translator, and editor, focusing on Indonesian and Javanese culture, for over 30 years.